The Iron Country

Introduction

The book you're holding began its life way back in 2012. One morning, sitting at the kitchen table, laptop open in front of me, I decided I needed a B-project, something I could flit back to when the A-project was doing my head in. Now this wound up being published first. Funny that... At least the irony isn't lost on me.

The Iron Country began life as a 6-page short story with zero direction outside of its initial concept and its opening scene. At the time, I bashed out something of a quick finale on the fly and called it done. I sent it out to a few magazines and crossed my fingers, filled with all the hope and zeal that only the naive can possess.

I was devastated when it was rejected by them all.

I went through all the usual stages of rejection. I was angry, then I was upset, then I was depressed. I had failed. I all but gave up, but something in me couldn't write it off fully. I kept being drawn back to it, compelled to do something with this one piece when I'd shelved so many others for less. About a year later I pulled it back out and realised they were right to decline it. I would've. It sucked.

I reworked it over the next year, but it still lacked direction. I told a friend (who has had the dubious honour of reading every single draft) that I was to completely rework the ending, because I felt it was too hollow and it lacked the impact I wanted the story to have. Then, months later, he received a version that had more than doubled in size. It was getting there. Then I added chapter 3 for good measure.

Six years, three house moves and two laptops later, here we are.

When the chair of the National Association of Writers Groups rang me and said I'd won first prize, the actual words I said to her were "are you serious?" For days I kept expecting a phone call to tell me there'd been a mistake, some kind of admin error. Then the certificate came in the post, so I guess that cemented it. I honestly never expected to hear anything back. I never do, so it's always a nice surprise when someone thinks I've created something they think is worthy of publication.

Through all this writing malarkey I've come to understand and appreciate the term 'labour of love'. It's something that's horrible, time-consuming, and if you're an overly critical sort like I am, it never ends. It means staying up 'til two in the morning when you start work at eight, avoiding social engagements and hiding yourself away from your loved ones every evening and day off to spend time with imaginary people. But at the same time, you can't imagine your life without it.

I hope you like this book. I don't plan to stop any time soon.

Sam Graham
February 2018

About the Author

Sam Graham was born and raised in Hull, Yorkshire, though he currently resides in Lancashire. He plays the guitar and occasionally walks up mountains for fun.
His favourite film is Blade Runner. His favourite drink is tea.

Follow him on Twitter: @samgraminc

Facebook.com/samgraminc

Instagram: the_abyss_looks_back

For Ash.

If it wasn't for you, this wouldn't exist.

The Iron Country

1

Jimmy was ill even before we'd broken out of the Workfarm, but the days on the road since had really taken their toll on him. He didn't see it at first- the thick glob of blood he'd just coughed up on his gloves, but when he looked around at us, one by one, and saw the same look on each of our faces, he noticed it. As he wiped the dregs off his lip, his chin started to quiver. I turned my attention to the fire before he could look at me again. I didn't have any answers for him. Ken did the same. Gina wrapped her arm around him and pulled him close to her as he sobbed.

"I keep telling you we should go up to Scotland." Gina said.

"And I keep telling you," I said as I stoked the fire with a piece of metal that used to be a chair leg, "we'll get nowhere near the border. We might as well turn ourselves into the Greens now if that's what you think, 'cause they're already all over the towns. What do you think the wall's gonna be like when we get there? If we get there?"

"Well we can't just stay here. They'll be looking in here before long."

Cheers for that, I thought. She just had to point out the obvious, like I'd been able to forget it. She loved doing it, I knew she did. She muttered something else under her breath, but I didn't hear what it was. I was a good thing I didn't too. I was already sick of it.

All three of them fell quiet as they stared into the fire and thought about Gina's words. The fire itself was going out. The room was pitch black outside the circle. All we had left were a few chunks of MDF from the desks. We'd already burned most of the schoolbooks, the drawings of Christmas trees and Father Christmas on the walls. Ken had found a couple of old guitars in the music room. They didn't last long. The MDF fumes stank. No alternative though. The place was supposed to be empty for the holidays, so putting the lights on would be a dead giveaway we were here. Breaking in was tricky, but nobody would notice one smashed window from a distance. It was low-key enough. We kept the fire small and didn't have it going for long. It did little to keep the cold off though.

Ken pulled his coat tighter around him and held his hands over the flames. He still had his gloves on. We all did.

"Where are we anyways?" Jimmy said. He coughed again. No blood this time.

"Reckon we're just about south of Burnley." I said.

"Exactly. And that's why we can't stay here. I'm not going back there for you lot." Gina. She couldn't go one minute without chirping in. I used to think it was just her Welsh accent that made her sound snotty all the time. I was starting to realise it was just her.

"We'll be gone before morning anyways, so don't you worry." I said. I made sure they both heard.

"How come?" Jimmy said.

I sighed. "Ken said he saw two Greens on the street out front earlier on. They were Hunters. They'll be breaking in here tomorrow I reckon."

I was surprised they hadn't already, but I didn't tell them.

"And when was you planning on telling us this?" Gina said.

"Just as soon as you let me get a word in, if you must know. We have to be out of here before daylight, preferably a couple of hours before, so don't mess around, any of you."

"So where are we going then?"

"Not north." I told her.

"Where then?"

"I don't know yet. I'm still thinking. There's got to be somewhere hasn't there? An empty house or something, not in any town? Somewhere the Greens won't think to look?"

"Like where?" She said.

"Did you not hear me say I don't know yet." I said.

"Oh great plan. Never thought of what to do after we got out. Brilliant."

"Well, what about the coast or something?"

Gina scoffed. "Oh yeah, let's go to the seaside everybody. You think they won't be there to see if we try and leave the country? Bloody hell."

"That's exactly what I've been saying about Scotland, but you weren't too bothered about it then, were you?" That shut her up. She didn't have a comeback for that one. Instead she slouched back and turned her attention on Jimmy. It wouldn't last though. Give it a minute, maybe two and she'd start up again.

"Why are they even after us? I mean, we aren't prisoners." Jimmy said. I was staying well out of this one. As I preoccupied myself with the fire again I glanced over at Ken. Seemed he didn't want to inform Jimmy either. Even Gina kept shtum.

Jimmy coughed again. It was another bad one. He doubled over and struggled to catch his breath between the spasms. Gina rubbed and patted his back until it was over. There was a lot more blood on his gloves now. As he wiped it off on his trousers I could feel him looking at me again. I pretended not to notice his sad puppy eyes and concentrated on stoking what was left of the fire, then I loosened the bandage on my left hand to keep the circulation going. It was hurting more since we'd broke out. I should take the bandage off and have a look at it, I thought, but I didn't. I didn't want to. Not with these lot looking. Gina put Jimmy's head on her chest and stroked his greasy hair. As she kissed his forehead, I sighed.

"It's nothing, Jimmy. Just a bit of dehydration, that's all. Have a drink and get some rest. You'll feel better." I said. I didn't know if he believed me or not. He probably didn't. I wouldn't.

Ken tossed another chunk of MDF on the fire and checked the water in the pan sitting on the tripod he'd fashioned out of chair legs. As he did he gave me a look, a stern raised eyebrow, a piercing gaze. If it meant what I thought it did, I'd been thinking the same thing all day.

I sighed again.

When the water was simmering I poured the instant coffee I'd found in the staffroom into the pan, then Ken broke out the plastic cups and the powdered milk from the kitchen cupboards and passed them around. It tasted bitter and cheap, probably been in the cupboard for years, but who was I to complain? First hot drink in months. I couldn't even remember the last one. It must have been the day the Greens came for me. I took another sip and closed my eyes and tried to enjoy it while the hot water settled in my stomach and warmed me up. Then Gina started again.

"It's not very nice this, is it?" She said.

"Sorry," Ken said. "I left my Colombian blend back at the Workfarm."

She gave him a big sarcastic grin and put her cup down in front of her.

"Thanks, Ken." I said as I went for a second cup.

We put the fire out with Gina's coffee, then turned in.

The tarp had come off in the middle of the night. It was still dark when the aching numbness in my hand woke me up. The cold had seeped in through the bandage and even the bones were numb. I tugged at the bandage, almost tearing it, panicking until it came free, then I held my mangled hand in the other one and blew warm air onto the stump. When the pain receded I got up and took one of the kid-sized chairs over to the window. My feet and remaining fingers had all gone numb from the cold and in the light from streetlamps outside, I could see my own breath. The others were still asleep. Gina and Jimmy were in the corner, propped up against the wall, his head on her chest and her arm draped over his shoulder. Ken had wrapped his tarp around him and had his back to us. I wrapped my tarp around my shoulders and rubbed my chest until I was warm.

A light came on in one of the terrace houses across the street. I watched a woman open her living room curtains and sit down with a mug of tea on her lap. She was covered in a thick, banana-yellow dressing gown and had white fluffy slippers on. It all looked so cosy in there. Just thinking about how it must have felt warmed me up for an instant. She flicked through telly channels for a while, then took a mince pie from the coffee table and downed it in three bites. A Christmas tree took up most of her window. I knew Christmas had gone, but I wasn't sure about New Year. They never told us what day it was. Then the woman picked up a laptop from under the coffee table and opened it up on her legs. It was similar to the one I'd had, before they'd taken me away.

Further down the road was a bus stop. A government poster on the side read: 'THEY PLAY, YOU WORK. NO MORE #nomore #workbackthedebt #feedthenation'.

Over the tops of the houses, I saw that the sky far off was turning orange. The sun would be up soon. Time to wake the others up.

We left the school later than I'd have liked, keeping to the backstreets, single file. Most of yesterday's snow had turned to slush and ice and a heavy fog had settled in, leaving us with only fifty metres or so to see. By the time we were out of the town the sun was already up behind the clouds and the wind was biting. The clothes they'd given us didn't do much to keep it off either. Full of holes and already worn down by god knows how many people before us. We shouldered into the weather and thanked god it wasn't snowing. Ken waited until we were on a quiet patch of country backroad that went towards Burnley before sidling up to me.

"There's another Workfarm over there." He said.

"Where?"

He pointed to my left across the field. "Just over there. See it?"

I did.

The spotlights were visible in the fog as lighter patches of grey. Through them I could make out trace silhouettes of the ten foot high fences topped with razor wire, guard towers, and the faint, dark grey haze of the main compound buildings.

"They'll already be out in the fields." I said.

"It's already halfway through the work day for them." Ken said. Most of the Workfarms were only a few miles away from each other. Close enough to the roads to be seen, but far enough away to not be given a second thought.

"Reckon they have any winter clothes?" I said.

"Did we?"

"Poor people." I said as I shivered.

"Hmm." Ken said, indifferent.

By now Gina and Jimmy were a good ways ahead. Christ, Jimmy looked worse than ever. He was delirious. Eyes half closed, veins blue in his cheeks. He wouldn't wake up at first. We thought the worst. Gina stayed with him and since leaving the school, she'd complained at us every few minutes to slow down and let him catch up. She was walking funny too. Agitated, like something was chafing. She'd said there were no towels in the school, so she was having to use the cheap, tracing paper toilet roll they had instead. I could have felt sorry for her if that was the only reason she complained so much.

Ken grabbed my arm and whispered: "He'll end up getting us caught. We should dump him. And her. She's got some mouth on her. And she'll use it too if we don't get rid of her sharpish."

So he was thinking the same as me.

"Come on," Ken continued. "He's dead weight."

"Yeah." I said.

"He barely says a word and hasn't contributed a damn thing. It was a fluke that landed them two with us in the first place. It was meant to be our escape, remember?"

Actually it was supposed to be my escape. Solo. Funny how plans change.

I sighed. We could move faster without them, but it was me who'd signed off on them coming in the first place. I'd freed these people. Me. I made it happen, not Ken. I didn't abandon them to the Greens. I could have, easily in fact, but I didn't. I'd had chances too. They were here because of me. That made them my responsibility. The second I'd said yes though, I knew that that solo road was one I'd always be looking back on with regret. Always questioning the possibilities. What if? If I was on my own then this wouldn't have happened. I could do this. I could go there. I wouldn't have to discuss it in a god damn committee every time and I wouldn't have to listen to Gina moan about it. It'd only been five days and I was already running out of ways to convince myself the grass was greener on this side. Right then though, at that moment, I wondered which choice would wind up being the biggest gamble.

I reminded myself again that I'd made the choice based on good intentions, but when were those intentions going to start paying off?

"We're not leaving them." I said. Ken tutted and walked on, muttering to himself. He could keep it to himself as well. I was in no mood for his shit either.

We followed the A-road, walking in the ditch on the opposite side of the trees. Good job too as after twenty minutes or so, four Green vans drove by.

"Get down." Ken said. The others crouched behind the bushes, but I couldn't move. I froze. I watched them pass us in single file. Massive things they were. Six-wheelers, covered in dark green metal plating, trailing diesel fumes behind them and carrying a deep thrumming engine that sounded like a tank. When they were gone I rested against a tree and tried to swallow down the feeling of inevitability that was rising up my throat. There were more of them where we were going.

Those vans were heading towards Burnley as well.

We stopped when the first few houses were in sight.

"OK, so what are we going to do?" I said. Nobody said anything in a hurry, so I did it for them. "We should split up."

Gina tutted. "Giving orders now?"

"Looks that way, doesn't it? I did ask for suggestions."

"Oh yeah, split up so you can pop off and have a chat with the Greens. Tell 'em where we are." Gina said. She pushed her hair back behind her ears. Her dark brown roots had grown out months ago and were longer than the dyed red ends now.

"And why the hell would I go and do that, you paranoid freak? Remember the time when I got us out of the Workfarm?"

And all you did was follow me.

"So why split up then?"

I rolled my eyes. "I'd have thought it was obvious by now."

Ken stepped in between Gina and me. "I think the idea is, the Greens are looking for a group of four. And we are a group of four. Does that make sense?"

Jimmy muttered something. Milky white saliva pooled at the sides of his lips, but if what he was saying were actual words I couldn't tell what they were.

"Are you two listening to him?" Gina said, one hand on Jimmy's shoulder. "He said he can't go on his own."

"Fine, you go with him then." Ken said before I had the chance to.

"He needs medicine as well, you idiots." She gave us both an angry look when we didn't reply. "Fine, I'll get it myself then."

"Where from?" I said.

"What do you care?"

"Just answer the question."

"I'll have to go to a chemist, won't I?"

"That's not a very good idea." Ken said. He held his hands up to protest and she stared up at him and snarled.

"There are a lot of cameras in them. We should try to avoid people. And the Greens will-"

"I have had enough of this. You two can just about go your own bloody way." Gina said. Her head shook as she spoke and she blinked between every word. "I've had it with the pair of you."

"Hey now." I said. "We need to help each other, or we're all screwed. Otherwise we're just as bad as they've made us out to be. It's fine. Gina, you go to a chemist if you want and get Jimmy some Calpol or something. Just don't try and blag anything prescription. Shelf only. We'll sort out food for tonight. We'll meet up after dark on the other side of Burnley."

"And what about when one of you doesn't make it?"

"We'll both be there. Come on, we're supposed to be a team."

"Yeah, but what happens when-"

"We'll both be there."

Gina thought it over for a moment. "I don't like this." She said.

I don't care, I thought.

She agreed and we split up just before we reached the first set of houses.

It looked like we were going north after all, but there wasn't a chance in hell we'd make it to the border, Gina.

2

Ken kept the girl talking while I browsed at the far end of the shop. He leaned his elbow on the glass counter like a man on the pull and gestured to the blue and red braids in the shopkeeper's hair. She was taken aback when he told her how lovely they were. I couldn't tell if it was genuine modesty or just good customer service, but Ken kept it up and asked her questions all about how and why she got them done. Good man, I thought, keep her busy, just like we'd talked about. She was young and looked just naïve enough to fall for it. As she was telling him about some model she'd seen with similar braids I started taking chocolate bars off the shelves and stuffing them in my pockets. I had to be careful not to drop any due to my missing finger. I wasn't choosy. You don't like caramel, Gina? Tough.

Next to the sweets was the newspaper rack, where the last copy of the Burnley Express caught my eye.

FARMING COMMUNITY OFFICER DIES.

The father of four, Adam Braithwaite, who was left fighting for his life after being beaten and mutilated by a gang of four, has passed away.

The attack came as a shock five days ago when, at the Government Sponsored farming community at Smithybridge, the group of four who are currently at large, asked to speak to Mr Braithwaite in his office, where they set up on him. Mr Braithwaite was rushed to Manchester Hospital with broken fingers, pulled teeth and severe internal bleeding where after five hours, was stabilised. However at 4:02am this morning his condition worsened and the doctors were unable to revive him.

"It's a terrible tragedy that this man who, through trying to help, has had this happen to him. It's a deep loss to the community." Said Scott Duffy of Cheshire Council.

"I just wish they understood the pain they've caused." Mrs Braithwaite said, tearfully. "Our littlest told me this morning he wanted Santa to take his Christmas presents back and bring back his Daddy. Poor little soldier."

The four offenders, unable to find gainful employment due to poor education and a lack of qualifications, volunteered to work back their debt to the nation as part of the Government's revolutionary 'Work Back To Work' program. Since the attack, they have fled the farm and are currently on the loose. Police have had reports of violent attacks and sexual assaults from the gang in the South Lancashire area. One of which included the rape of a fourteen year old girl.

Greater Manchester Police have issued a reward of £5000 for any information that can lead to the capture, and arrest, of these individuals.

I almost laughed. I would have done if I didn't realise the implications. It didn't surprise me that they'd try something like this. If anything, I was surprised at how unsurprised I was. I rolled up the paper and stuffed it down my sleeve. The others would need to see it. They needed to know what we were up against. I thought this kind of stuff only happened in films. There weren't any other reported breakouts from the farms, so as far as

I knew we were the first. But if that article told me anything, it was that what people knew wasn't always what had happened.

Why they were even letting people know there'd been a breakout at all?

Ken was still listening to the girl. The subject had changed to fine art, which apparently she was doing her A-levels in. Ken dropped the names of a few artists I'd never heard of and this seemed to spur her on. She lit up and got more chirpy about it. I left the shop when my pockets were full and waited round the corner. Ken looked awful chipper when he came out. A smug little smile at the side of his lip. Awful proud of himself, he was.

"Manage to get her number?" I said.

"I wish."

"Dirty old man." I said. We laughed, but when I handed him the newspaper his smile dropped. After he'd skim-read the front page he nodded, then gave it back. I put it back in my sleeve.

"Lays it on pretty thick doesn't it?" He said.

"Yeah, especially that bit about the kids. I don't remember volunteering for life on the Workfarm, do you?"

"No. And who's this Braithwaite bloke? I don't think I met him."

"No, I don't think any of us did. Funny that. We killed a man we've never met. I like the part about what we did to him too."

Detain if need be, but we hurt nobody- That was the rule. I'd made them all swear to it.

And nobody was hurt. No people anyway.

"Doesn't matter though. People will believe it. And they'll have pitchforks and flaming torches at the ready too." Ken said.

"I can imagine the comments sections now."

Ken nodded.

"What are we going to do about it?" I said.

"Nothing much we can do. We can't change it."

"True. They'll have all read it by the end of the day." I sighed. "Come on then, we'd best get a shift on. Oh, here, have this now before we meet up with them two." I gave Ken a KitKat. I was saving anything with caramel in it for later.

The four of us stopped for the night beneath an overpass where a dual-carriageway crossed over the M65. The sky was the colour of a cement slab. Somewhere on the other side of it, the sun was on its way out.

"Any chance of getting a fire going?" I said to Ken. He was a scout leader in his prime- his words- so when it came to this stuff, he was more qualified than me. He looked up at the thick clouds, then at the long line of barren trees by the roadside.

"Not really. Wood's all wet from the snow. And really, a fire out on the motorway is a bit too easy to notice don't you think?"

"Good point." I said. We climbed up the cobbled slope and sat down in a circle with the crossing road inches above our heads. Gina rolled her eyes as I dumped the contents of my pockets on the ground.

"What's this?" She said, looking disgusted at the spoils.

"A slap up carvery. What does it look like?" I said.

"Piss off. I told you I'm allergic to caramel."

"No you didn't." I said. "You said you didn't like it. That was all. We've all had to put up with things we don't like. If it was a medical thing, you should've said."

"Well I'm telling you now. I can't eat caramel. It's a medical thing."

"I don't believe you. Beggars can't be choosers, Gina. Eat. You don't know when we will again." I unwrapped a Mars bar and stared right at her as I took a bite. I was so sick of the taste of sweets. The cloying in my back teeth. That limescale coating it left on my front ones. Sugar had become bitter. It gave me stomach cramps now. Any other time I'd have listened to Gina moan all day for some sausage and chips, but right now I wanted to eat this whole pile of chocolate bars and have her watch, just out of spite. She had a nibble of a Snickers, then made out like she was choking on it. She was no actress either. Then she broke a Galaxy Caramel into bits and fed them to Jimmy, one segment at a time. She even made sure he chewed it before swallowing. There's a good boy. Jesus Christ.

"Thanks." Jimmy said after a few segments.

"It's alright." I said. "Did you manage to get any medicine?" A car went over the road right above us. It rattled the whole concrete slab, but wasn't as loud as I thought it would've been.

"No." Gina said with a mouthful of Bounty. I'd forgotten to eat that one before we met up. Damn. "Too many people around the chemists and CCTV all over the place. Saw some Greens around too. Had to go around." She carried on chewing.

"You mean, exactly what we told you there'd be?" Ken said. She stuck her middle finger up at him and when she'd swallowed the chocolate, opened her mouth again. I got in first.

"Hey, pack it in, the pair of you. Just leave it for one night. Just for now, neither of you say anything." I said to them both. They just shrugged and looked down at the food.

To take their minds off of each other I showed them today's paper.

Traffic died out on the motorway as the night came in. The few cars that commuted on the orange-lit road had already passed by before they had the chance to notice us. I couldn't sleep. None of us could. It was far too cold for it. I sat at the top of the concrete slope, legs hanging down, coat pulled tight, shivering. I'd taken the bandage off my hand to let the air get to the stump, but the cold only made it hurt like an open sore. It didn't look like it was healing right, if it was healing at all. There were bits of black on the skin between the stitches. It didn't smell of anything, but it still shouldn't have looked like that. The antibiotics were back at the Workfarm too. The escape route didn't go by the storage lockup. Too dangerous. It was right next to the Greens' rec-room. Looking at it now, the poor thing looked pathetic. Incomplete. Useless. I could wiggle the stump, but that was about it. Making a fist didn't feel right without the little finger to keep it taught. It just wasn't the same. And now every time I looked down at it, or went to pick something up, I'd be reminded of the time I'd said no to the Greens. If just saying no got me this, then what the hell would escaping the farm get me?

Damn those Greens. Those bastards...

My fingernails had turned blue from the cold, so I wrapped the bandage up and put my gloves back on. On the billboard across the road, Prime Minister Tony Bennett stared at me. I deliberately looked past him, at the lights in the distance. Some of those lights would be Workfarms. They'd have had their evening meal by now and it would be about time for final roll call before lights out. While we were lined up, the Greens at the Smithybridge camp would ask us a question each from a Trivial Pursuit box. They used to say they were responsible for keeping our minds healthy too. A wrong answer meant no breakfast in the morning. Three wrong in a row meant recalibration. I'd seen men and women break down when they got that third question wrong. Some put on a brave face and let them get it over with. One woman begged for the Greens to let her off and ask her another question. She never begged again after that.

And to think I complained about eating chocolate every day...

Ken sat down next to me and we split a miniature bottle of Jim Beam I'd found in the teacher's cupboard. Gina had taken Jimmy off to the far side of the concrete block. She had her arm around him and it looked like she was whispering to him. Something was going on with them two. Something weird. I wanted to keep an eye on her, but then Ken started up.

"They'd organised a search group, this bunch of idiots in my area." He said. "Called themselves the EEC. Apparently it stood for the Employment Enforcement Crusade. That's what their Facebook page said anyways. They went around dressed up like a bloody militia. Balaclavas and army jackets, stopping people on the street, going door to door and shouting through people's letterboxes, demanding the people inside prove they've got a job. Nobody ever answered them. People thought they were a joke. They'd put videos of themselves on the internet walking around and screaming in people's faces. 'Patrols'.

"Then one afternoon they saw this fella on my street. They followed him back to his house and broke in. Dragged him out in the middle of the square. Then a bunch more of them came with cricket bats and knives and did the same thing to the whole street. Four of us were rounded up. They forced us into the middle of the road while they called the Greens to come pick us up. Their van showed up, same types we saw this morning. The Hunters didn't even say a word. They just corralled us into the van. They even let some of those idiots help. They didn't speak to any of them either. But," He paused for a moment, sobbing. "they took Sam. He kept trying to climb up in the van with me and there were all these bastards in balaclavas standing in the way, waving good riddance to us, laughing, calling us parasites and workshy scum, waving handfuls of money around, kissing it. One of them was Abigail Harrison. She only lived six doors from me. I couldn't believe it. I'd looked after that bitch for months when her husband died and there she was, spitting at me... I even let her take Sam for a few days for some company... Last I saw they were dragging him away from the van by his collar. They've probably put him down if they didn't... As soon as I was gone..."

He was sobbing in full force now. I didn't know how to comfort a crying old man, so I passed him the bottle. He took a deeper swig than I'd have liked before passing it back empty.

"They didn't say anything to me either, Ken. I've heard a few people say that, you know? Everyone I talked to at the farm said the Hunters don't talk. They don't even speak to each other. Not sure why. It's strange. They don't speak, you can't see their faces... God knows how they communicate. I was in the shower, so I never even heard them come in. They pulled the curtain back and three of them dragged me out. I didn't know what was going on. They had hold of my arms and legs. One of them gave me this," I patted the back of my shoulder, on the scar shaped like the pointed end of a crowbar. He'd seen it before. "then I don't know what happened, because I woke up in the back of the van. At least you weren't in the buff.

"I never thought they'd come for me though. I don't know why, I just thought it wouldn't affect me. You don't though, don't you, whenever stuff happens? It feels miles away. I thought they had more important people to go after. I mean, I was only out of work for a few weeks. I had interviews lined up. I tried to tell them..." I sighed and blew warm breath onto my fingers. I needed a drink. "God knows what we're gonna do next, Ken. Claim squatter's rights somewhere maybe? I dunno. We can't just keep plodding on out in the open like we have been doing. There's got to be somewhere, just, it's not in Scotland. I'm sure of it. Besides, do you really think we wouldn't get deported back to England?"

Ken shrugged. He wasn't really listening. Probably zoned out ages ago. Too busy thinking about his dog.

"A sign earlier on said Nelson's the next town up, but do we really want to keep going up that way? What do you reckon?" I said. I threw the empty bottle at the Prime Minister across the motorway, but it didn't even get halfway across before it smashed somewhere on the hard shoulder. Ken still didn't say anything, but he'd stopped crying. I looked over at him. He was staring up at the night sky, eyes wide with terror, his jaw clenched tight.

Then I heard the rotor blades, and I did the same.

It was the Greens.

The spotlight travelled fast up the road, swathing though the darkness, sweeping left and right, illuminating both lanes.

"Hide." I managed to shout before the sound of the rotor blades drowned everything out. Ken and I ran down the slope to the nearest support pillar while Gina and Jimmy crawled into the bushes at the edge of the overpass. She wrapped her arms around him and pulled him tight as the helicopter's light stopped on the road above us. It paused and hovered over the middle of the road. The spotlight panned left, then right, then it crept up the concrete slope as the chopper descended. It engulfed the spot where we were sitting just a few seconds ago. Ken pressed himself so close against me I could smell the week-old sweat on his clothes. We both made sure no bits of clothing were sticking out the side of the pillar. Nothing they'd be able to see with infrared. If they saw even so much as a finger, that would be it. The Hunters would be on us in minutes. I didn't even want to think about what would happen to us between now and the five o'clock start at the Workfarm.

The spotlight edged closer. Ten feet away, then eight, then five. I was shaking. Terrified to tears. The beam crept over the cobbles, about to expose us. Inches away now. Run, I thought. Just run now before the damn thing lands on you. Get a head start. They can't catch you now, not after everything. Not after all the days on the run. You don't deserve it.

Run.

If Ken didn't have me pressed against the pillar, I might have. The sound of the rotor blades was agonising, but I couldn't cover my ears. The light passed right over the pillar we were hiding behind, then across the other side of the motorway. The helicopter jinked to the right to get a better angle of the underpass and turned its light towards us again. Now they would see us.

This was it.

Then suddenly, half way across the motorway, the light stopped. It jolted and wavered, then hung there for a long while. Then it retreated into the middle of the road and the chopper went back up.

Ken and I stayed still. They still had infrared. As the helicopter flew over the road, the spotlight cascaded across the billboard on the other side. The gigantic Tony Bennett on it stared at me. His slogan 'It's Gone On Long Enough #getthemworking #fighttheembargoes #workfarm' in big white lettering was the last to fade.

We waited until the chopper was half a mile away. I couldn't bring myself to move at first, but I had to. I was too close to the road. I climbed back up the slope to the concrete plateau and sat down in the same spot as before. Gina and Jimmy were already back at the other edge. I offered Ken a hand, but he managed on his own.

"Thank god for those power lines." He pointed at where they crossed over the motorway. "If they weren't there, it would have seen right underneath here."

"We got lucky." I said. I called over to Gina and asked if they were alright. She had her arm around Jimmy again. She looked at me, but didn't say anything. I turned back to Ken. "It's a sign, Ken. We can't stay out here anymore. We can't do it. It won't work. They're ramping up the search." My voice was trembling. I cracked open the last miniature and necked it all in one go. It didn't stop me shaking.

"Well, have you had any thought about what I said this morning?"

I knew this was going to come up again.

"About what?" I said.

"That there're too many of us." He whispered. "Too large a group."

"Yeah."

"There're too many horns clashing."

"Yeah."

"And it's only going to get worse the longer it goes on."

Even though the light was gone I could still feel the Prime Minister staring at me from across the road, reminding me he was everywhere. Pockmarked cheeks on a bitter man's face. Eyebrows crushed together in an anger that he'd infected a nation with. The embargoes were his doing. He'd tried to act like he fought against them, but it was his actions that brought them on in the first place. Villages and towns up north were the first to feel it, but it wasn't until the shortages hit London that he unveiled his great solution. A few headlines here, a few celebrity endorsements there, and before long people were agreeing with him. With no trade coming in, the unemployed were eating the country out of house and home and they weren't giving a thing back in return. The shortages were all their fault. The Workfarms were the only solution.

Now he'd set the choppers on us. What else did he have? How much more could the four of us avoid?

I sighed. Ken was right. "Yeah."

"Come on," Ken grabbed my arm. "The kid's done. And her... Well, she spits her dummy out soon as you look at her."

I didn't say anything. He wasn't exactly wrong.

"They're liabilities. We can't be done with liabilities. Look at today. She nearly made an unnecessary trip to a chemist. I sincerely doubt she wasn't noticed. Anyone could've reported her to the Greens. That kid over there's done too. He will be soon anyways. Better to spare ourselves the trouble of having to deal with him now."

"Didn't you used to be a teacher?" I said.

"So? What's that got to do with anything?"

"I dunno, I just thought maybe-"

34

"Maybe what?" He leaned over me. I could smell the whiskey on his breath.

"I thought maybe you'd be a bit more humanitarian."

He scoffed and gave me that look that teachers give to kids when they want them to own up to something.

"Jimmy's an adult." He said.

"Barely. I don't think he's even shaved before."

"He's the same as the rest of us. He made his own choice didn't he? Chose to escape didn't he? It's time you kids realised that once we got over that wall, we were on our own. Every one of us. Each. Singular. We owe each other nothing."

If he really believed that shit then why was he so interested in me pairing up with him and not just going off on his own?

"How do you know they're not over there discussing the exact same thing?" I said. I looked over at Gina and Jimmy again. His head was on her lap now. I couldn't tell if he was awake, or even alive, given the state of him earlier, but I could hear her whispering to him. I'd liked to have known what she was saying.

Gina stopped talking when she saw me watching. She turned back to Jimmy and stroked his cheek with the back of her hand. I didn't know what their relationship was exactly. At first I assumed it was sexual, a bit weird considering the age difference, but it didn't seem to be that. She nursed him like she was his mum. I didn't much care until recently. Whatever it was, it was their business. I hated that it was becoming mine.

God, I should have gotten out on my own. It would have been so much easier.

"We could kill them." Ken said.

"You fucking what?"

"Come off acting like you hadn't thought of it. You've still got that knife haven't you?"

It wasn't a knife. It was a tooth broken off a rake that I'd taped to a toothbrush. And it still stank of blood.

"Jesus, no I'm not killing anyone."

"Give it here then."

"Get lost."

"You've got no bottle, boy."

"Fuck you, old man."

"Oh drop the morality will you? It won't do you any favours when she gets you caught. You made short work of them dogs, didn't you?" He was raising his voice a little too high. I heard Gina shift and turn around.

"That was different." I whispered.

"Was it now?" He leaned back on his elbows and leered at me in a smug, condescending truthfulness that only booze brings out in people. He'd only had half a miniature too.

"It was." I said. "And look, I told you all straight up that if you're coming with me, you do it my way. That means no hurting anyone. The second we lay a finger on someone, we've become what they say we are. We've given them licence to hunt us. If you can't handle that then that's your problem, mate, but that's all there is to it. End of discussion."

He responded by telling me how pathetic I was and storming off to the back of the flyover. He sat down against the concrete wall at the opposite side from Gina and Jimmy with his hood pulled right up so I couldn't see his face.

I wondered what made him suggest such a drastic option? He'd been on the farm longer than most of us. He'd seen things, I suppose. Kept himself to himself for the most part. But still...

I threw the empty bottle down onto the motorway and heard it smash. Stupid old bastard. Suggesting I murder them. Why did I have to do it? The dogs were different. They were an obstacle on the way out of the compound. And I'd tried to make it quick for them. I really did. Did he think I wanted to do it? To hold their mouths shut while I drove the rake tooth into their throats? Hold them and stroke them while they slipped away. Their growls turned to whimpers turned to silence. The first one was hard enough, then four more right after. And it wasn't until two days ago that I finally had the chance to wash the blood off my hands.

Ken wouldn't help, oh no. Too much of a dog lover. Too busy thinking about his precious Sam. There was still some of it under my nails.

That was why he stuck with me. I was the one who'd step up. For all his talk, I was the one who would do something. I got us out, not him. Stupid old man. And after all I'd been through for him. All I'd lost.

I ran my hand through my hair as I tried to think, but nothing came.

Christ, I wanted to go home.

Yeah right. Don't kid yourself. Someone else will be living there by now. You don't have a home. Closest thing you've got to a home are these people here.

Great.

Another helicopter, maybe it was the same one, passed by about a mile away. I sat up for another hour or so watching it. It never stopped looking for us.

3

The storm had turned the fields into sludge overnight. The mud squelched and sucked at our feet and we sank in up to the ankles as we headed out for morning roll call. We lined up near the barn we used as the store, just in front of the fields and looked over the mud. Pools of brown water swamped the whole farm. Orange and brown autumn leaves had blown in and mixed in with the bog.

The lines were decimated. The onions we'd spent the last few weeks planting in prep for winter were ruined. There was no way we'd be able to get any work done today. God knows what they expected us to do. We'd be grafted in minutes with no progress to show for it. Shower day wasn't until Wednesday either. Doubted they'd do a one off. Got to save water, apparently.

A couple of guys further down the line laughed, then more joined them. The ruined lines were a small victory for us, even though we had nothing to do with it, but it was a spanner in their works all the same. Anything that interfered with their plans, or pissed them off was a win for us. They all shut up pretty quickly though when Officer McCarthy stormed out of the office building. The door banged against the concrete wall then rocked back on its loose hinges. McCarthy's thick moustache, carefully trimmed into a Kitchener, seemed to resist the wind as he huffed and panted his way through the mud in his knee-high wellies and dark green uniform. His shoulders hunched, red faced, he muttered to himself and shook his head as he marched towards the line. Whatever it was, he was too mad for it to just be about the lovely weather we'd been enjoying.

Something was wrong.

"Right, ladies and gentlemen." He shouted. "It's come to our attention that there's been some vandalism on the grounds."

The line stiffened. All notion of a small victory disappeared.

"One of the rakes is missing some of its teeth. May I remind you that this equipment is not provided by us. It's paid for by the hard work of the taxpayer. It's the best, most durable that money can buy, so that you can work as efficiently as possible, for them, and for your country. It does not break on its own. One of you lot has done it on purpose. Now you listen, all of you, and listen good. Due to the embargoes, we and the other farms have an entire nation to feed. Every man, woman and child in England, Wales and Northern Ireland lives off the produce grown here. So when you break the taxpayer's investments, you put the people's lives at risk. Children eat, or starve at your hands. Something must be done, and something will be done today." McCarthy paused while he let that last part sink in. He paced up and down the line, fancying himself a drill instructor, staring down every one of us, inspecting us for signs of deceit.

"So before we start this morning, we're going to play a game." He held up a thin black box, opened it, and ran his finger along the hundreds of cards inside. Starting at the left-hand side of the line, he asked questions from the Masters Edition of Trivial Pursuit. The first guy, Ben Owens his name was, got his question wrong. McCarthy's moustache curved upwards like a pair of horns as he smirked. Ben wasn't unemployed before he wound up here. He was a small-time journo for the Filey Mercury. Printed one article slamming the Workfarms too many and when one ended up being the most retweeted post that week, he ended up on the telly about it. His rants got personal on morning TV when he slated Tony Bennett's family, namely his wife's billionaire dad, who coincidentally was the party's biggest contributor. A few days later he disappeared. He'd said the Greens at the Workfarms must be 'the highest paid professional sociopaths since Patrick Bateman', which had rubbed McCarthy the wrong way ever since he arrived.

Standing behind him, Barker and Payne grabbed Ben and dragged him into the store. McCarthy took a step to his left and waited in front of the next person on the line, Lyndsey. I didn't know her too well. The Green looked down at her, then along the line. He wanted to make sure we were all listening to Ben, and the recalibration going on in the store.

When Barker and Payne emerged, dragging Ben by his shoulders, his face was bloated and bloody. They dumped him back in his spot on the line and got behind Lyndsey, ready to do the same. McCarthy asked Lyndsey the next question. She got it wrong.

Lyndsey was the one who begged. Only the once though.

It carried on like that, going down the line one at a time. The farmers outnumbered the Greens at least four-to-one. They knew it, same as we did. They had truncheons and the ones in the towers had rifles, but we had the numbers. Only problem was, the morning porridge, two bowls of tinned meat and veg a day and five hours of sleep each night didn't give us the energy for a full day's farming, never mind an insurrection. Deprived of sleep and on the edge of starvation, we were thinned out and cut down to nothing. Some of us lost hair, a few lost teeth. Some of the women dropped weight so quick their monthlies stopped. Before this, a friend used to tell me I wasn't shy of a few pies. Now I could feel my ribs through my jumper. We were skin and bone within weeks.

Twelve in and so far not one question right. Ken was up next.

"Now then. Got one special for you, Kenny my boy." McCarthy said with a smirk. He didn't take any cards out of the box. "How can you lift an elephant with one hand?"

"Fuck off." Ken said.

"No, I'm afraid the answer is elephants don't have hands." McCarthy gave the nod to Barker and Payne. Before they could grab him though, Ken hooked McCarthy in the chin. There was an audible gasp from the line as McCarthy staggered and wiped his lip. The momentum from his swing left Ken on his knees, and Barker and Payne got hold of him to keep him there.

"Oh you've done it now, sunshine." McCarthy said. "You." He pointed at me, then to the patch of mud in front of Ken. "There." I moved. "Give him ten."

"Ten what, boss?" I said.

McCarthy knew full well I wasn't as daft as I was making out. He grabbed my jumper and hooked me the same way Ken had him. I fell in the mud. After the initial dizziness passed and my jaw clicked back into place, I stood back up. "Ten of that. Go on. Now. I'm counting too, so you'd better keep pace."

I rested a hand on Ken's shoulder. He didn't look up at me. Didn't acknowledge me in any way. He just stared solemnly ahead, unwavering, refusing to give the Greens anything, refuting their authority.

I made a fist.

"One."

I tried to make it look like I hit him hard, but McCarthy grabbed hold of me again. "Do it properly. Do it right, or I'll get the whole lot them to do it to you." He stepped back, then shouted: "I want to hear it. One."

"I'm sorry, Ken." I said. I did it hard. McCarthy heard it. They all did.

"Two... Three... Four... I said four... Good. Five..."

The force of each impact jolting up my arm was nauseating. It wasn't the pain itself, but the awful feeling of power that came with it. I'd never hit anyone up 'til this point. Never been in a proper fight. Never been beaten up. Now here I was battering this bloke because of something he'd done to them, all because I was afraid of what they'd do to me if I refused. Ken didn't make a sound. He didn't wince and he didn't try to stop me. He took every punch. He wasn't afraid of them and that was the difference between me and him. Ken couldn't be broken. It was a strength I didn't have. I admired it. The Greens knew I was afraid of them, and using that fear, they'd made me into their tool. They couldn't do this. We outnumbered them for god sake. And from what McCarthy had said, they needed us more than we needed them. They had no right. All it would take was a few more people to show them that. If Ken could do it, then so could I.

"Six... What do you think you're doing?" McCarthy said as I wiped the blood on my trousers and stood back in line. The skin on my knuckles was red raw, but I didn't let the pain show. I kept repeating the words 'If Ken can do it, so can I' in my head. Ken finally dropped down into the mud.

McCarthy was gobsmacked. The level of insubordination he'd witnessed this morning was unreal. A personal insult to his authority as Farm Overseer. No one else had said no to them, far as I knew. He watched me face forward with the same refuting look as Ken. An amused smirk spread across his face as he wondered just what the hell was going to happen next.

Down the line, most of the other farmers were the same. Hard faced, emotions turned inwards, away from the Greens. Some watched, disgusted, while others kept their eyes closed, trying to pretend it wasn't happening.

McCarthy laughed. "Well well well. I'm half expecting some of you to tell me your name's Spartacus next. You think this solidarity is going to win the day? That you can't be hurt if you all band together like you are doing now? It's very cute."

As Ken was dragging himself to his feet, Payne kicked them out from under him and said: "Back down, you. Still got five more to go yet, lad."

McCarthy looked at me, nodding in agreement.

"Come on, Spartacus. Get it over with. We've got a special question for you next. Reckon you'll love it" Payne said.

I told them I wasn't doing it.

"I beg your pardon?" McCarthy said.

If Ken can do it, so can I. If Ken can do it, so can I.

They'd heard me fine the first time. They just wanted to see if I had the guts to repeat it. If Ken could do it, so could I. I shouted that I wasn't doing it for the whole line to hear.

46

McCarthy looked along the line again. Nothing happened. Nobody moved. No great revolution broke out. The wind blew, the crows squawked, and a pair of boots squelched in the mud as Barker moved behind me.

Next thing I knew my face was in the mud and my hands were being cuffed behind my back. Payne and Barker started dragging me to the store, but McCarthy stopped them.

"You're all going to watch this." He shouted to the line. His nostrils flared in anger.

Barker held his truncheon across my throat as Payne undid the cuffs, then refastened my hands in front of me. McCarthy took a pair of secateurs from his pocket and clamped my little finger in them. He turned his back to the line and whispered in my ear: "Just say you're sorry and give him his five, son. Believe me, you don't want this to go any further. There's no going back from this. Don't make me do it, please. Just give him his five and let's be done. There's a good lad."

This had to be just for show. He wouldn't actually do it. They'd be shooting themselves in the foot for handicapping the workers. I'd let people know. They'd have to take me to hospital and I'd tell everyone there what happened. Payne had to hold my hands still because they were trembling so much. My heart beat so fast it ached. I looked down at Ken. He was already wincing.

Why wasn't he doing something? The whole line was watching. The urge to do something was on all of their faces, but none of them were willing to actually do it. What was the point in them? They were useless. Just hit Ken five more times and be done with it, I thought. McCarthy doesn't want to do it. He said so. See, he is human. He doesn't want to seriously hurt anyone. His authority has been challenged, that's all. He just has to reaffirm it. Just give him what he wants. Give Ken his five and it's over. Them lot aren't going to do anything anyway. They won't help. They're all too afraid. They don't even care, because it's not them. They'll just watch, looking all 'downtrodden silent majority'. Too afraid to do jack shit. Can't help themselves, won't help themselves, none of them willing to be the first one. Followers. Good for nothing followers, the lot of them. Ken can't do it, neither can they, and neither can I. I'm screwed. Jesus Christ. Jesus fucking Christ.

"See, Spartacus." McCarthy said. "You're on your own."

He closed the secateurs. He had to use both hands to get through the bone.

The doctor arrived twenty minutes later. No ambulance though. He parked up on the gravel road in a Citroen Picasso. He was a Green doctor in a Green uniform. There wasn't going to be any trip to the hospital. I wouldn't be able to tell anyone.

Nobody would ever find out.

I should have just given Ken his five.

4

Ken planted his hand on my shoulder and dug his fingers in as he whispered "It's your show, mate. How are you going to run it?" in my ear.

Yeah cheers, I thought as I saw how many Greens there were in the centre of Nelson. They were crowding around a group of protesters in the main square. They weren't Hunters. Just uniforms. Some coppers mixed in with them too to bump up the numbers. Hunters wouldn't be far away though. They never were lately.

Nelson was one of those grey industrial towns. Mostly old buildings. Probably built on an industry that died out a few generations back. Nothing to do. Nowhere to go. Nothing but the people left here to justify its existence. The snow had melted earlier that morning, but the clouds threatened to bring more of it and while it was only just gone noon, it already looked like it was getting dark. Traffic through and around Nelson was gridlocked because of roadblocks. Greens were looking inside cars one by one, wanting to see faces and licenses, looking for us.

The centre of Nelson was a long stretch with shops on the right hand side and the broadside of an old building to the left. Lines of bollards and trees and benches on either side. The protesters were massed in front of the library at the farthest end. There were only about fifteen of them, and they weren't really doing much, but I guessed it was enough activity in a small town like Nelson to warrant the authorities' presence. One of their signs read 'WORKFARM CAUSES HARM' and another had a drawing of Tony Bennett eating tiny people off of a silver platter. A big, fat, gold-toothed smile on his face. They held their pickets up and shouted at the top of their lungs. A couple of them stood apart from the group, live-streaming it on their phones. The louder they got, the closer the police and the Greens got. A lot of commotion for a small town centre. Lots of eyes watching. It would only take one to recognise us. We couldn't go around though. Too many roadblocks.

"Hey, where are you going?" I said as Gina started taking Jimmy off down the street to our left.

"We're going this way. Meet you on the other side, like yesterday." She said over her shoulder.

"Hang on, we didn't discuss this."

She stopped and turned around. "And I'm not going to. You can't make our decisions for us."

Not this again.

"How are you planning on getting through then?" I said.

"None of your business."

"And just why the hell isn't it?"

"Where are you really going?" Ken said with that teacher's down-talk again. "What were you two talking about last night?" He pointed at her and Jimmy, who was in no better state than he was yesterday.

"Nowt for nosies." Gina said.

"You're up to something, Gina. You and that whelp." Ken said. He stepped closer to her and stuck his finger right in her face. He towered over her by a good foot and a half. "What is it?"

"Oh piss off you, you paranoid old sod. You think I wanna risk taking Jimmy through all that lot?" She gestured to all the Greens and the protesters.

"It's not like you can just avoid them, Gina. You saw the same as I did coming into Nelson. It won't work. Unless they'll let you go past, that is. Awfully cagey about yesterday as well, weren't you? I know you're hiding something."

I grabbed hold of Ken's arm and pulled him back. "Just let them go, Ken. Go on then. Do what you like. See you later."

Gina huffed and stormed off with Jimmy. We both waited until they'd turned the corner and gone out of sight.

"What are you doing, boy?" Ken said.

"I'm sick of it, Ken. I don't want to be around her."

"You realise they could be selling us out?"

I nodded. Maybe, but what were the chances? She probably just wanted to get away from Ken. After last night I couldn't blame her. So did I. A gust of wind cut right through my clothes and made me shiver as I coughed into my gloves. There was dark yellow phlegm on them. No blood though. That was something at least.

"Reckon it'll do anything?" I asked as we crossed the road.

"What?"

"The protest."

53

Adrenaline built up as the whole square waited for whatever was about to happen, to happen.

Heads turned when one of the uniformed Greens cried out. He collapsed to the ground, holding his stomach, bleeding, stabbed by one of the anti-Workfarm lot. And there it was: the spark to set it all off. In the moment that followed, the protesters dropped their pickets, broke past the circle of Greens and scattered. The police and the Greens gave chase. The leader of the EEC let out a cry and they rushed forward, and the Hunters started running.

Looking back, I don't know why me and Ken ran too. After all, their attention wasn't on us. But after seeing the writing on that picket, it was a bet they'd know our faces if they looked hard enough. All it would take was one passing glance. One tiny bit of recognition. One voice to shout out over the many, then we'd have everybody's attention, and they'd all have that five grand reward on their minds.

We ran to the end of the square, across the road and carried on until we were a few streets away. I could still hear the commotion, mostly from the EEC. They were chanting something, but I couldn't make out what they were saying. It was probably best I didn't know.

We didn't get much further before we both ran out of breath, so we stopped in an alley behind a Wilkinson. There was a pain in my chest that wasn't just from the running. I leaned against the wall as I coughed up some more dark phlegm on my gloves. I wiped it on the wall before Ken had the chance to notice. A moment later someone else came running down the alley. He stopped when he saw us. He was young. Early twenties. Blonde hair. A bit overweight. He looked smart though. I recognised him as one of the anti-Workfarm protesters. I gestured for him to come and hide with us and Ken told me to stop and ignore him.

"He's on the run too now. Besides, he was protesting against all this." I whispered.

The protester came over.

"What's your name?" I said.

"Marc." He said as he rested his hands on his knees and caught his breath.

"Well Marc, we're not safe here. Take a sec and catch your breath, but we've got to keep going on."

He looked confused. "Hang on, you two aren't part of the protest." He said. "Why are you running?"

I told that we only ran, because everyone else did. I told him to stick with us, because we could get him out of town until the heat died off. He went along with it and agreed to come with us. I

He laughed. "Not a chance."

"It's good that they do though, I suppose."

"There were protests when Tony Bennett won the election and when he first proposed the Workfarm scheme. Didn't stop them from happening."

"It raises awareness though."

"It doesn't make any real difference. Besides, it's not as though people don't already know about it. They either just pretend they don't, or they don't care."

As we neared the commotion, the Greens and the police were closing in around the protesters, forcing them shoulder to shoulder in a little bunch. They'd quietened down now. I whispered to Ken that we should circle around them. We were almost clear when a voice shouted from behind us. It was joined by a chorus of other voices that cut through the sound of the protest, and we and everyone else in the square turned to see a group of thirty or so men dressed in olive coats and black beanies. Raw, angry faces shouted as they held up pickets of their own. Their signs were something straight out of the EEC Facebook page. They marched towards the anti-Workfarm protesters, staring them down like they were about to go to war.

I took a step back, away from the crowd when I read one of the group's pickets: 'LIFE DEATH 2 THE SMITHYBRIDGE 4'.

The coppers turned away from the anti-Workfarm protesters and formed a line between both groups. They knew, just as well as everyone in the whole square knew, that it was about to get ugly.

But when four Hunters turned the corner right behind the EEC, the police all but stepped down.

The anti-Workfarm guys bolted as soon as they clapped eyes on them. It became clear then why the Greens were encircling them. They couldn't get away. They were boxed in, stopped from running before they could even start.

Sure, there were only four Hunters, but that was enough. Four hulking suits of Kevlar plating. Black bodies with military green shoulders, arms and legs. Each one of them wore a black mask that obscured everything. Their eyes were blacked-out rings, no mouthpiece to speak from. Nothing but a few ventilation holes on both cheeks. Each carried a truncheon in their hands.

There was a moment where both sides of protesters stood facing each other. The sense of anticipation was heavy. The police and the Greens stopped. Even the passersby stopped.

could feel the look Ken was giving me the whole time without having to see it. Tough. If Ken was coming with me, then he was doing it my way.

We left Nelson town centre and the streets became a maze of orange bricked terraces with front doors that opened directly onto the pavement and trees every few houses down. More than half of these old houses were empty. Boarded up. Since the embargoes, abandoned areas like these were common. Vast swathes of cities were becoming empty derelicts, their residents relocated to a Workfarm a few miles away and their kids in foster care. Villages, rural areas and big city centres were doing alright though. Anywhere that had money was thriving, what with thousands repaying their debt to society and the embargoes keeping it necessary. I was surprised there was anyone still Nelson from the look of it.

"So, what was the protesting for?" Ken said to Marc as we walked.

"'Cos it's not right what they're doing, innit? These Workfarms, they're against human rights."

"I think you'll find that law was repealed actually, but never mind. So what was the plan then? Protest and do what?" Ken said. He was doing that teacher's voice again. He looked over at me, making sure I was aware he was trying to make his point from earlier.

"It's to let the government know that people won't stand for it. There're photos on Twitter and Instagram, it's being live-streamed on YouTube, all the local MP's have been tagged in it. We're getting the message out that the people have had enough." Marc said.

"OK, Wolfie." Ken said, trying hard not to smirk. "So you're not going to stand for it, but what are you going to do to change it? The government can just ignore protests, you know. They have been doing for years. What makes this one any different from the rest?"

Marc struggled to answer. "It uh, raises awareness, for one." He didn't sound too sure of it now he was under the microscope.

"People already know about it, son. Besides, you just got bullied off by the opposition, and now you're running off with us. Christ-"

"Ken." I interrupted.

"What?"

"Leave it out. Let's just get out of here."

Ken sighed and muttered under his breath, just like he did last night when he suggested we murder two people.

"Why do I have to leave town again?" Marc said a few minutes later.

"You really think the Greens will let you go for this?" I said.

"You stabbed one of the uniforms. Even if it wasn't you, you were part of the group." Ken said.

"So?" Marc said. I thought then that maybe he wasn't as smart as he looked.

"So, you idiot, you're accessory to the crime. I saw you back there filming the whole thing on your phone. You were filming yourself as well. Like you said, you were live-streaming it."

"Yeah, so?"

"So now the Greens will know you're involved. They have your face. They'll trace it back to your Facebook, so they'll know your name, where you live, every little thing you've bragged about and taken a photo of. They'll hunt you down for it now. Hell, you're probably higher up the list than the Smithybridge Four now." Ken said. It felt strange hearing him refer to us like that. When I'd read that picket, I knew it was about us, but I didn't associate myself with it. It wasn't about the real us. Just the version that the papers talked about. In my mind I'd kept us and the Smithybridge Four as two separate things. When Ken said that though, it made it real. It made me realise I was one of the

Smithybridge Four whether I liked it or not. Regardless of what really happened.

"OK, so why are you two leaving? We're out of town now. Can't you go home?" Marc said.

I looked over at Ken and he gave me the same look right back. Seems neither of us had a good enough lie to tell Marc, so I pretended I didn't hear him for the wind.

The trouble started when he asked again.

We'd just turned a corner onto another terrace when Ken grabbed me by the shoulder and dragged me back behind the house.

"Hunters." Ken said.

"Shit." Marc said, panicking. He started back the way we'd just came.

"Stay here, Marc. Trust us. Just wait while I take a look."

A Green van like the kind I'd seen heading to Burnley was parked up at the far end of the street. Four Hunters were going down the terrace, two on each side, knocking on doors one by one. They made people stand outside their homes while they searched it, and crowbarred their way into the empty ones and the ones that didn't answer the door. It might have been the same ones as before, but who could tell? From the way they were canvassing the street they weren't looking anywhere specific. They were probably looking for us though.

"You still haven't told me why you two are leaving town." Marc said, and then, in his eyes, I saw the penny drop. He was confused and worried and terrified all at once.

"You're them who broke out." He said.

"Yep." I said. I turned back to Marc.

"The Smithybridge Four?"

"Yeah."

"Oh my god. Oh my god, you killed that man." He edged away from us.

"No." I cut him off. "We haven't hurt nobody. That was all just made up. Everything you've read about it isn't true. I thought you knew that anyways? You were protesting against all that sort of stuff."

"But you hurt those kids."

"Listen, you cretin. Those kids don't even exist." Ken said.

"Do we really look like the sort the newspapers say we are?" I said. "Didn't we help you? Aren't you here right now, because we helped you?"

It wasn't sinking in. The terror in his face grew as he recalled every vile fact he'd read about us. I dreaded to think what else we'd allegedly done. Marc backed away from us, around the corner, out into the street.

"Don't you dare." I said, but it was too late. He shouted as loud as he could.

"Here! Over here! I've got the Smithybridge lot! They're right here!"

Ken tried to grab him, but he was already running towards the Greens. The Hunters were looking this way. They'd seen him pointing. They were coming for us.

Ken and I ran back the way we came.

Ken stopped at an empty house we'd passed a couple of streets back. He cracked the front door window in the bottom corner with a stone, then potted the rest of it and climbed through. I followed him through to the kitchen, then out to the backyard, shutting the doors behind us. Ken climbed inside the black wheelie bin and closed the lid on himself and I panicked as I realised there was nowhere for me to hide. The yard was so tiny, it was just a place to keep the bin. No recycling bins and no room for two in the black one. No time to go back through the house though. I could hear them coming down the street. I crouched down underneath the large kitchen window by the door and pressed myself flat against the bricks, the top of my head only an inch away from a cluster of frozen cobwebs and a plant pot riddled with dried up stalks.

I heard the front door splinter and slam inwards as the Hunters kicked it open. They entered the house. By the footsteps it sounded like two of them. They walked cautiously, treading as light as possible in boots, securing the living room, on alert in case they'd been lured into a trap. They didn't speak to each other. The Hunters never spoke. They had to be communicating with each other, but nobody knew how.

Judging by the wooden creaking, one of them was heading upstairs while the other made its way into the kitchen. The footsteps paused as the Hunter surveyed the room. Then they stalked up to the back door. I held my breath and pressed myself again the wall. There were only a few inches of brick between us. All he had to do was open the back door and that would be it. I'd be going back to the Workfarm.

There was no way I was going back to that Workfarm.

The shank was in my hand. That rotten, nauseating feeling of inevitability was lead in my stomach. It had happened. We'd finally run into them. Another thing I was too arrogant to plan for. Oh no, I'll be so careful. They'll never find me. Well done. Maybe if I'd got out on my own they might not have. I wondered if Ken would help me if it happened, or would he sit stashed away in the bin until they'd carted me off? He'd better do something. He owed me.

The Hunter was moving around the kitchen, opening the cupboard doors and the fridge-freezer. His truncheon tapped against his thigh in a heartbeat rhythm, then the footsteps stopped. Breath hissed out of the sides of his helmet, making a sound like a hydraulic machine. I wanted to look, but I there was a feeling in the pit of my stomach that the Hunter was right by the window, looking out at the yard.

There was a step closer to the back door. A hiss on the window pane.

I closed my eyes and gripped the shank tight, praying, so scared I felt sick.

Another step. Another hiss. The Hunter paused again. Did I make a noise? What was going on in there?

The footsteps headed back into the living room. A moment after, I heard the front door close.

Thank god.

I stayed clutching the wall for a few minutes while I calmed down, then I gave Ken a knock on the side of the bin. I asked if he was OK as he brushed himself off. He looked down at me, sighing and shaking his head like this was all my fault. He nodded to give me the all clear, but he didn't bother to ask if I was OK in return. I was sure he could see that I wasn't. Oh yeah, I bet it was nice and comfy for him hiding away in the bin. He wouldn't have been the one spotted and he wouldn't have done anything to help, oh no. I didn't say thing about it though. Now wasn't the time.

We headed back through the house. The Hunter was gone. Likely gone further down the street. They'll have known we couldn't have gone far. Ken rummaged through the kitchen cupboards for scraps to take with us while I went through to the living room. As I rested my head against the wall I heard a creak on the stairs behind me. Something pinched in the back of my shoulder and before I could react, I was on the floor. Every inch of me was in pain, shooting through me from the thing stuck in my shoulder. My arms and legs constricted. My fingers contorted and my jaw clenched so hard my teeth whined. I couldn't breathe. The pain was screeching inside my head. Then, just as I was on the very edge of passing out, it paused. Only a second's respite. Just long enough to take a breath and stay conscious, then the Hunter squeezed the trigger and his taser carried on pumping me with voltage.

It was over then. They'd caught me.

The shocks stopped. I heard running. The floorboards creaked as heavy boots moved up the stairs, then across the landing.

Standing myself up, shivering, I pulled the taser barbs out of my shoulder. Had I eaten, I'd have thrown up.

"Ken! Ken run!" I shouted, but he wasn't in the kitchen. There was banging upstairs. Something slammed against a wall.

Ken.

I limped after him. More sounds of struggle from the upstairs landing. Skin impacting on skin. Ken groaned. Just what was he supposed to do against a Hunter? What could either of us do?

The stairs turned left at the top. The Hunter's helmet was on the floor. The two of them were in the bathroom at the far end of the landing. The Hunter, unmasked, was on one knee and Ken held a cistern lid in his hands. He raised it above his head and swung. There was a loud crack as the Hunter collapsed. Teeth landed on the hardwood floor in a streak of blood. The Hunter whimpered as he tried to shield his face with his arms. Ken broke them both with another swing of the cistern lid. I flinched at the sound of bones splitting. The Hunter's cries were cut off as Ken swung again. Even after he went limp, Ken carried on.

All I could do was stand there and watch.

"Come on. We have to run now thanks to your little friend." Ken said as he marched down the stairs. He left the cistern lid on the floor. I went over to the Hunter, making sure not to step in any of the blood and the pieces of him that had flayed off. I didn't know what I'd expected underneath all that padding and plating. You hear stories, conspiracy theories and all that junk about why the Hunters don't speak. Some of them are ridiculous. He was just a man. He looked like everyone else. No ID on his uniform. I wanted to close his eyes and stop them staring at me, but I was too afraid to touch him. This was going to change everything. Some protester stabbing a uniform was one thing, but this... This was unprecedented. It was terrible.

Ken shouted for me from the front door. Before I left I pulled the shower curtain down and laid it over the body.

5

"Will you slow down a minute?" Gina shouted. I turned back to her, grabbing her wrist and yanking her so hard that Jimmy fell out from under her arm and onto the pavement. Gina shook herself free and went back to him.

"We have to go right now." I said through clenched teeth, wanting to shout at her, but not wanting to draw attention to us. The four of us walking down the side of an A road was doing enough of that. I looked over my shoulder at Ken. He made a gesture like he was checking his watch.

"Well you'll have to wait." Gina said. She helped Jimmy to his feet.

"Look, I don't have time for your shit, Gina. We can't wait. I've told you. There's no time. We've got to go now."

She ignored me. Too busy whispering to Jimmy as she helped him up. He whimpered like a dying dog.

I swore at both of them and turned around. I can't believe this, I thought. Where's the urgency?

I turned back to her. "This is serious. Just listen for once." I said.

"Oh yeah, yeah. You two killed a Hunter. Course you did." She said, giggling.

"You saw the blood on Ken's hands. How can you still be so thick about it?"

She didn't say anything. Ken came over and eyed them both. "Just how did you and your patient there get past the Greens exactly?"

Gina looked down at Jimmy, then back at us. She opened her mouth to speak, then stopped herself. Ken smiled as though she'd just answered his question.

"They'll be after us with a vengeance now. This, all of them in Nelson, is nothing. It was a chopper last night. They'll have bloody tanks next for all I know." I said. "So get up and get moving."

"Where?" She said.

"I've already told you. We find an empty house."

We marched. Gina walked the rest of the way in silence. She didn't even talk to Jimmy. Wouldn't look at him either. It worried me that she was concerned about something else, but there wasn't time to think about that now.

The next town wasn't far, although I didn't see any signs saying its name. The first houses we came to were detached, two-storey affairs. Pebbled driveways and well preened bushes. BMW's and Merc's parked up at the front of the gates, Golfs and Punto's right behind them. Houses for the kind of people that would never see the inside of a Workfarm. The third one on the left was all dark. No cars, no curtains in the window and no lights on. It looked right, so I got them to stay back while I crept up the driveway alone and peered through the front window.

The room was bare and empty. A small living room for such a big house, but it was a good sign. It would do. I signalled the others to come up and we crept around the back. Gina volunteered to climb over the fence and unlock the gate, but I said Ken was going, because he was the tallest. He managed to climb up and over on his own, using the drainpipe for leverage.

The bolt squeaked. Once we were all in the back garden I moved the wheelie bin in front of the gate to keep it shut. It saved us having to use the bolt again and risk waking the neighbours. Jimmy was another problem though. When he wasn't coughing his lungs up he was wheezing so loud and so hoarse it sounded like agony. Nothing I could do about it now though. Just mentioning it would only start Gina off. She'd barely taken her hands off him since Nelson. She was practically carrying him now.

The grass in the back garden hadn't been trimmed in months. Another good sign. The back door window was split into six small panes which made it easier to smash the bottom corner one with a rock, then work my hand in to unlock it. We kept the lights off, making our presence known as little as possible to the neighbours. That was until Jimmy slammed the back door. I was ready to go for him. He just stood there shivering, arms wrapped round himself, looking sheepish and innocent. Useless was more like it. Gina got in front of him and whispered that it was a draft. Fine, whatever, I thought, I'll deal with it later. Deal with them both.

Through the kitchen was a second, much larger living room. Carpeted floors and a staircase on the right hand side. A short hallway at the far end lead to the front door and the smaller living room. Something was off about it though. The house was warm. Even in the dark it felt cosy. I couldn't figure out what it was until the landing lights came on, then the answer was all around me. Framed photos on the walls, the green light blinking on the router in the corner, the cold, half drunk cup of coffee on the table by the couch.

Shit.

Bare footsteps came down the stairs. I froze. With any luck they'll go back up and we can leave without them noticing, I thought. But when Jimmy coughed, the person on the stairs shouted for his mum to call the police.

Ken was straight on it, already heading up the stairs. I shouted for him to come back, but he didn't listen. The guy at the top of the stairs yelped as Ken pinned him to the wall and clamped a hand over his mouth. I ran up after them, past them, to find the woman.

I found her sitting up in bed, legs out the side, dialling on her phone. I threw myself on her and got my good hand over her face. The phone dropped and she screamed into my glove. She was strong. I only just managed to push her down on the bed as she punched and scratched at me and bit into my glove. One of her fingernails caught the stump on my left hand and as I winced from the pain, she managed to shove me off. The moment she was free, she reached for her phone. Her screams for help were bound to alert the neighbours, so I got my arm around her throat and dragged her back down on the bed. Climbing on top of her, I sat on her chest and planted my knees on her upper arms to take away her leverage. Then I covered her mouth and nipped her nose shut. When she realised she couldn't breathe she panicked. I pressed all of my weight down on her and pushed down on her head as hard as I could to stop her fighting back. Tears streamed down her face. Eyes full of terror looked up at me, scared to die, yet scared of what might happen if she lived. Then, in my hands and underneath my legs, I felt her go limp as she blacked out.

Ken was already dragging the unconscious boy into the bedroom. I made sure the woman was still breathing, then climbed off her and covered her up where her top had slipped during the struggle. Ken lifted the boy on to the bed.

"Right, we need to get out of here while we can. They won't be out for long." I said. I was shaking, out of breath. My finger stump was on fire. It felt like it was bleeding again. I checked the woman's phone and the call hadn't gone through. In fact the phone was off, because there was a big dent in the glass that had fractured the whole thing. Good. "We should never have come here."

"And the second they wake up they'll call the police and sic the Greens on us." Ken said. Gina walked into the room with Jimmy in tow.

"We can be long gone by the time they wake up." I said.

"It won't matter now. Like you said, we killed a Hunter. I reckon we should stay here for a while. Stick to the plan. At least here we're out of the cold. And I don't imagine the Greens are going to start hunting in a posh area like this, do you?"

"No, no, no, this is wrong. The plan was for an empty house. No hurting anyone I said. I told you all and you all agreed. Look at this?" I pointed at the unconscious two on the bed.

"It wasn't us who chose this house?" Ken said. "This has always been your show, boyo. You made that pretty clear last night. And as for not hurting anyone, where would you be if I didn't sort out that Hunter?"

I wished he would stop talking.

I turned to Jimmy. "This is all your fault. You and that god damn cough."

That set Gina off. Then Ken started up again: "So come on then. Let's all go back out into the freezing cold and if we don't freeze to death, there'll be helicopters and Hunters chasing us down every street. Because when they find that body, you can expect martial law.

"Try to understand and imagine what they'll do to you when they catch you. None of us will make it back to the farm. The second that Hunter died, we woke the beast. This became about survival."

"Yeah, and who brought that on us?" I shouted.

"You did when you trusted that protester and got yourself caught." He shouted back, louder.

I had no comeback for that.

All three of them stared at me. Anger etched into their emaciated faces. This was my show. I'd got us into this mess. I looked down at the two lying unconscious on the bed.

"This wasn't supposed to happen." Christ, I wanted to throw up.

6

I let the water trickle down my shoulders and my back, all the way down the backs of my legs to my feet. I stood under the shower head until the hot water ran out, then I turned off the taps until the boiler refilled and did it again. The bathroom steamed up and it smelled like strawberry shower gel. I smiled as the warmth radiated through me, soothing away all the pains and the stiffness. It reinvigorated me and just for a moment- just for one small moment, I forgot all about the last week and the months at the farm. This was such a luxury. Something I once took for granted, that I used to think of as a chore on days when I was in a rush, was now such a sweet thing. A special, sacred thing. I revelled in it. I laughed. Then I cried.

When I was done, the bottom of the bath was coated in all the brownish-grey muck that had come off me. It took some scrubbing to clean up, then I soaked my damaged hand in warm water in the sink. From the stump to my knuckle was black and felt soft to touch. Flakes of the black skin scrubbed off and stained the water. There was blood in it too, but not much. After that, I cleaned it up with a bottle of iodine from the medicine cabinet and put on a fresh bandage.

I came down the stairs feeling a bit like my old self. Clean, hair washed, shaved, the chill pains were gone and for the first time in months I was in clean clothes. I went straight into the living room, where the owners of the house and the clothes I was wearing were tied up and gagged in front of the fireplace.

Ken had tied them up with a roll of duct tape he'd found in the kitchen cupboards. He'd bound their hands and feet together and taped them together across their chests so they were sitting up back-to-back. There was tape over their mouths too.

It's only temporary, I told myself, just until I can talk to them, get them to understand. I hadn't explained it well with Marc. I didn't have time. With these two I did. I had to get them to understand.

It was just gone six am. The fifth of January according to the calendar. It was pitch black outside and snowing. The wind battered against the windows. Definitely not a time to be out in it. The woman on the floor was stirring. If they were mother and son, there couldn't have been more than two decades between them. He was about sixteen, I figured. There was a school uniform in his room. A few wisps of hair on his chin and spots on his cheeks, but he was lanky. His jeans and hoody were baggy on me. A gas bill said the woman's name was Natalie Monroe. There was nothing with the kid's name on it. I guessed there was no dad around either, because only two of the four bedrooms had actual beds in and the only men's clothes were in his room. The other rooms upstairs were a study and an Xbox room. I'd tried using the kid's laptop, but there was a password on it and when I found his phone I smashed the screen and hid it, more to stop Gina or Ken using it than anything else.

It took Natalie a moment to realise where she was, then it all came back to her in one painful rush when she saw me standing over her. She whimpered. Her sobs stirred her son and it was a damn good job we'd taped his mouth shut, because he started screaming the second he woke up.

I knelt down in front of her.

"Natalie." I said. She flinched away as I tried to get her to face me. "Natalie, listen to me." She kept her eyes closed. Her son wasn't helping either, struggling to get loose. There was no way I'd get her to listen while he was making so much racket. He needed to be calm. Everybody needed to be calm.

"Ken, could you tell him to be quiet please?" I said. Ken nodded and took a pair of scissors off the table. He held the kid by the throat and put the tip of the blade to his stomach.

It stopped him, but I hoped Ken understood it was just for show.

"Natalie, listen to me. Listen. We won't hurt you. We're not here for that. I'm sorry we're even here at all, but it was an accident."

Her whole body trembled as one tear-filled eye opened.

"Natalie, I'm not a bad person and I'll prove it to you." I took the tape off her mouth. She coughed.

"What do you want?" She said.

"Just to talk."

"No. Why are you in my house?"

"Like I said, it was an accident. We won't be here long. I promise." I said. I dried her cheeks with my sleeve. Again she flinched.

"I know who you are." She said.

"Who are we then?"

"You're the ones from that farm place."

I nodded.

"You killed that man."

"No. We never laid a finger on anyone."

"It was on the news the other day."

"I know. I read it in the paper too. Braithwaite isn't real, Natalie."

"You would say that."

"Only because it's true. None of that stuff is real. They're lies to turn people against us. I've seen it."

"You expect me to believe a word you say with all this." She looked down at the tape on her hands.

I didn't say anything.

"So what do you want?"

"I thought your house was empty. We needed somewhere for the night. Honestly, we'd never have broken in if we knew there was someone in here. That other room over there looked empty." I said.

"So you're saying this is my fault for wanting to redecorate?"

"I'm just telling you how things looked. Like I said, we aren't going to be here for long, but we can't trust you. That's why you're taped up."

"That's a load of crap." She rested her chin on her chest. "Are you going to..." She sobbed.

"What?"

"Take me to the bedroom for it, alright? Not in front of my son, please. I won't resist. Just don't hurt him."

Her son started wrestling again. Ken squeezed his throat.

"Leave him alone." Natalie said.

"Not until he learns to calm down." Ken said.

"Let him go. Please, he's not going to do anything."

"Not a chance. We can't just let you go now, can we?" Ken said.

"Please." She said.

"You're safe with us, Natalie." I said. "Nobody's gonna hurt you and that's not going to happen. We just... Look, it was an accident, OK. We're just trying to survive."

"You're all bloody scum."

Ken looked at me.

"Are we really?" I said. "For what, trying to survive? Trying to get away from all that shit? Shit you don't even know about. Just look at my hand, Natalie." I showed her. "Just what crime did I commit to deserve this?"

"You fucking kidnapped me." She screamed. She cried for help. I rushed to get the tape over her mouth and as I leaned in, she spat at me. Without thinking, I hit her hard across the cheek. I didn't mean to. It was a reflex. A snap reaction. Then I grabbed her by the cheeks and squeezed them together to stop her screaming.

"Don't you spit at me again. They took it from us, just like we came in here and took it from you. Does that make you a criminal as well? I didn't think it did."

"Well it just proves them right about you, doesn't it?" She said.

I pressed the tape back over her mouth up and went into the kitchen to calm down. I leaned against the sink and sighed. My hand hurt from when I'd hit her. It was my bad hand too.

The back door was right in front of me. It was still dark outside and would be for a few more hours. Ken was talking to Natalie and her son while Gina, who was laid across the couch the whole time, took Jimmy upstairs to get some sleep. I could leave now and put this whole mess behind me, I thought. They're all preoccupied and they wouldn't notice. Go it alone like I should have done all along. Make my own way without the baggage. Go where I want to go.

Which is where exactly?

Out the window the snow was blowing sideways and battering against the glass. Beyond it were the spotlights from three different helicopters in the sky. One was coming this way.

We'd woken the beast. They were relentless now.

I let go of the idea, knowing it would never happen, that it was pointless and naïve of me to have ever thought so. Ken proved that when he took care of the Hunter. I didn't help. I couldn't have. I was useless. If I was on my own, that would have been it. I screwed up. I screwed up a second time with this house as well. Maybe I was the baggage.

I sighed again.

"I didn't mean to do that, Natalie. I'm sorry. It was an accident."

She said two words underneath the tape.

After closing his eyes and savouring that first sip, Ken told me he'd forgotten what a cup of tea tasted like. For a moment, all the strain and worry was gone from his face and he smiled in a way I'd never seen before. We downed them as soon as they were cool enough, then made another round straight away, then a third to accompany a full English. Ken put his away in minutes then opened a packet of Hobnobs as he stood watching the sunrise by the back door. I ate so much so fast it gave me stomach ache. I wasn't used to it any more. Smoked bacon, Cumberland sausages, tomatoes, fried bread, button mushrooms, baked beans, rosti, all fried in the same pan so the juices mixed together. Looking through the fridge and the freezer, I thought of all the meals I could make. There was enough for at least a week. The shortages hadn't hurt the Monroe household, it seemed. I offered to make Gina and Jimmy something, but she said she'd sort themselves out once I was done. Ken, still looking out the back door, muttered to himself. Gina and I both looked at him, but said nothing, then she turned back to me and said she was going upstairs to check on Jimmy.

I took a bag of Skittles into the living room. Natalie glared at me as I sat down in the chair and put the telly on. Her cheek was still red. "I'll make you something in a minute, don't worry. I just need to check something first." I said as I flicked through the channels and stopped on the news. They were talking about us.

"Rhodes' body was found yesterday evening in the bathroom of a derelict house in Nelson. The police suspect the Smithybridge Four, those responsible for the murder of Adam Braithwaite, to be responsible. Since the murder at the farming community, the four have been on the run ever since, and it looks like they are travelling North up the motorway. Here's Tom Sykes with more information."

"Thank you. I'm here at the Government-sponsored farming community just outside of Smithybridge to see what the fellow farmhands have to say about their former colleagues."

"Well it's just terrible, isn't it? They came to us looking to make a difference and improve their lives and this is how we get repaid."

"Thank you. And do you know them personally?"

"I knew one of them a bit. He came across as a bit of a layabout, y'know? Didn't want to get his hands dirty. Thought farming would be all pushing buttons or something, I dunno. He was barmy. Reckon they must have all had a screw loose."

"And can I ask, how has this opportunity to come here to the farm helped you, sir?"

"Well, it's been a good opportunity, like you said. It's a nice feeling, to be giving something back to a society. The country needs me more than ever now. Those European lot need their heads bashing together and actually start listening to the Prime Minister and lift those daft embargoes. Little ones need feeding. So I help produce the food for people to eat, and that's worth all the hard work at the end of the day. And, you know, it's taught me a trade, given me some valuable life skills that can hopefully lead to employment elsewhere."

"Do you like it here?"

"Very much. I don't want to leave."

"And the staff here?"

"Oh they're a cracking lot. Very helpful. Accommodating. Here comes one now actually."

"Where do you want them?"

"Oh just put them over there with the rest. I'll put them away in a minute."

"Will do, boss."

"Sorry, you were saying, Tom?"

"Yeah, they seem like an easygoing sort. Good for a bit of banter. So, given what you've said about this farming community, can you understand why anybody would want to leave?"

"No, not really. I can't."

I turned the telly off and sat still while I tried to comprehend what I'd just seen. The Skittles I'd been chewing on since Sykes came on were stuck in my throat. I glanced over at Natalie who frowned at me.

"That's not Smithybridge." I said. "There's no barn like that there. And I don't know who that guy is. I know everyone at that place and he isn't one of them."

She shook her head. She probably thought I was barmy too.

"He's an actor. That guard's an actor. That's all staged. That farmer, he wasn't shy of a few pies, was he? Do I really look like I eat as well as him?" I lifted the hoody up and showed her my chest and my ribs. I pointed to the bruises. "That I got for not getting enough rows hoed. That one I got for being late for evening roll call. That one I got for answering back to the Greens." Then I showed her the hand again. "And this they did just to prove a point. We've all got them. Every one of us. And not just us four either. There're around two hundred workers per farm and we've passed at least six of them since we broke out. You figure it out."

The look she gave said I deserved everything that was coming to me. I walked away.

After I finished the Skittles I cooked up two more breakfasts, took them both into the living room and placed them on the coffee table. I knelt down by the kid and took the tape off his mouth.

"I want my fucking clothes back now." He said the instant his mouth was free.

"Can't do that I'm afraid. Open wide." I said as I dragged a slice of bacon through some bean juice and held the fork up to his mouth.

"You've poisoned it or something." He said.

I ate the bacon off the end of the fork and got another bit ready. "Want to try that again?"

He ate it that time, but his eyes never moved off me. So much hate smouldering in them made it difficult to look back at him. Judging by the way he kept sniggering at me, he knew it too.

"What's your name?" I said as I offered up some sausage and egg white.

"Jonathan." He ate with no hesitation.

"Well Jonathan, I wanted to ask you-"

"When are you going to fuck off?"

Behind him, Natalie murmured through the tape.

"Soon." I said, regretting starting the conversation with him.

"How soon?"

"As soon as we've decided on a few things."

"Like what?" Jonathan said as I gave him a second load of sausage and egg.

"Private stuff. Stuff to do with us. Don't worry, we're not gonna hurt you."

"Yeah? Then how come we're tied up?"

"So that you don't hurt us."

"Course it is, yeah. 'Cause you know I'll turn on you in a fucking heartbeat if you ever let me go. Touch my mum again and you're dead."

I slammed the plate down. "Look, do you want feeding, or don't you?" I waved a forkful of rosti in front of him. He didn't say anything, but as soon as the food was in his mouth he spat it back at me and started shouting for help. I clamped one hand over his mouth and the other around his head to stop him thrashing around. I called for Ken as he bit me between my thumb and forefinger. Ken rushed over and pried Jonathan's jaw open enough for me to get free and he screamed again.

"I'm trying to help you, you idiot." I said as Ken put the tape went back on. My hand stung and there was blood around the teethmarks and on Jonathan's lip. I hated the way he kept staring at me. That cocky little smirk. I wanted to wipe it off his face. All that hate made him incapable of seeing reason. In that moment, I truly believed he would kill us all if he ever got loose.

"Don't do that again. We're in charge, remember?" I said as I wrung the pain out of my hand. His meal was over. I picked up Natalie's plate and took it around to her while Ken sat in front of Jonathan and finished off the rest of his breakfast for him.

"Do I have to prove to you it's not poisoned as well?"

She shook her head.

"Can you be quiet? Are you hungry?" She nodded. "I honestly just want to talk, Natalie."

I took the tape off her mouth. She kept her word and stayed quiet. She licked her dry lips and took a deep breath while I got some egg on the fork for her. She shook her head. "What's the matter?"

"I don't eat the white."

I rolled my eyes and gave her some bacon instead.

"You know, if you tried the food at the Workfarm, even for one day, you wouldn't mind the white."

"Don't talk to me like we're friends. Just do what you need to do and get out. We won't call the police, I promise."

I dropped the fork on the plate and sighed. "Are you going to start shouting now as well?"

She shook her head again.

"Let's try and keep it civil then shall we? So what do you do?" I said as I fed her some beans.

"I, I work for the council."

"Yeah? What's that like?"

"Same as any office work really."

"Looking around your house I'd say you do bit more than your average office work. You're not suffering from the shortages I see."

"What's your point?" She said.

"Oh nothing. Just good to see you doing so well while there are thousands of people on Workfarms, that's all."

"I'm not responsible for the Workfarms, or the embargoes, you know. And I'm not Tony Bennett, so don't take that class warrior stance with me. You don't know anything about us. You're just going off what you see right in front of you."

"Is that a fact?"

"It is. All you see is a big house and a single mother who must have lots of money stashed away, so I'm obviously hoarding it all to myself just to keep it away from the more deserving. I must be one of 'them'. Am I right?"

I paused for a moment as I thought of what to say. She wasn't wrong. She'd thrown me off and it hurt to have it pointed out to me. I wasn't aware I thought like that.

"It's not my fault you ended up where you did, and you're not my responsibility either, so justify this however you like. It's still kidnapping" She added. "And don't look all sheepish like that. You wanted us to talk, remember?"

I was mad at myself for starting this conversation and for letting it go this way. If I was only going off what I could see, then so was she. We weren't criminals, because we'd done nothing wrong- up till now anyways. I didn't say it though, much as I wanted to. It'd only escalate things again and I was too tired for that. But she did need to understand a few things though.

"You know, I used to have all this sort of stuff." I nodded towards a blurry photo framed on the wall of a teenage Natalie on a tennis court. Next to that was a framed Masters certificate in environmental management and another photo of her and Jonathan on a beach when he was a few years younger. "I was two years into a fifteen year mortgage, I had a fifty inch flatscreen, which is bigger than yours, and I had a six year old Yaris. I used to cook and I played cricket every other Sunday. I was doing alright."

Natalie ate some bacon and tomato. She looked impatient for me to get to the point.

"Anyway, the college laid me off a few weeks before the new term started. Said they were streamlining the department and I was the least senior staff there. It was only admin, but still... I tried to be optimistic about it, as you do. I had some savings and it was nice to have all that free time, but then one day the government stepped in and, well, here I am."

"What's your point?" Natalie said.

"Well, I was going to ask you, because I asked myself this a lot on my first week at the Workfarm. I had all that stuff, right? I worked for it and I paid for it all with my own money, so it was my property. Then the Government comes in and takes it all away from me, just like that. So, I've been wondering if any of it was ever really mine to begin with? I don't think it was now. It was all just borrowed. All the stuff in this house is borrowed. It's not even your house. They could just as easily come and take it off you tomorrow."

"No they wouldn't. I pay taxes. I contribute to society." She said.

"That's what I thought too."

"I'm not one of you people."

"Not yet you're not. All it would take is a little push." I said.

She looked disgusted. She whispered "Monsters."

"You still don't get it do you?" I tossed the plate on the coffee table. She flinched as it clattered and the cutlery rolled onto the carpet. I rolled my eyes and sighed. It wasn't working. I wasn't getting through to either of them. I never would. We'd come into their house and tied them up. We didn't deserve their trust. Over by the kitchen door, Ken was giving me his teacher's 'I told you so' look.

As I was putting the tape back over Natalie's mouth she asked me how long we were planning to stay. I told her not long. We'd be discussing it today. Right now, in fact. I called Ken and Gina into the empty living room. I noticed Gina wasn't walking awkwardly any more. She must have found some sanitaries in Natalie's bathroom. Like me, she'd also cleaned up a bit and changed her clothes. She was wearing some of Natalie's. They were about the same height, but Gina was much thinner.

"So, we need to discuss where we're going to go from here." I said. "And before you say it, Gina, I've made up my mind. I'm not going to Scotland. Not a chance in hell."

She took it as well as expected. "Well I suppose that settles it for all of us then if your mind's made up? You can toddle off on your own if you like, but I'm taking Jimmy there."

Great. One sentence in and already a pissing match.

"Woah woah, hold on a minute." Ken said. "Why are we in such a rush to leave? We've got the house. Full fridge, warm water, soft beds. It's the best we've had since before the Workfarm."

"Yeah, and it's also someone else's." I said.

"And like you said to that woman last night," Ken pointed at me. "We took it from them. It's ours now, and we should keep hold of it."

"No, it's not ours, because the owners are tied up in the next room. Jesus, what do you plan to do about them?"

I knew as soon as I'd asked. Wouldn't be the first time he'd suggested it. Wouldn't be the first time he'd actually done it. He didn't have to kill that Hunter. That first swing of the cistern lid would have done enough for us to escape. The rest he did on his own volition. Even in self defence, it was still murder. I could almost see the suggestion forming on his lips.

Gina interrupted before Ken had chance to say it. "And may I ask just what's so bad about Scotland?" She had her arms folded and leaned on one leg.

"Well, just after we got here I saw at least three Green choppers in the sky. We killed a fucking Hunter yesterday, Gina. Have you forgotten? Am I the only one that can see the implications? It's too dangerous now. Not to mention it's still god knows how many miles away and it's freezing cold."

"But we can't stay here either?" Ken said.

"No, we can't." I said.

"So where then?" Gina.

"Yes, where then?" Ken.

That question again. It had become a joke.

"Oh, and if we are to leave, and go back out there into the cold and almost certain capture," Ken had one arm under the other and he was waving his index finger around like he was enjoying this, "what would you suggest we do with the prisoners?"

"Yeah, we can't just untie them." Gina said.

"Well what would you do?" I said.

"No, I asked you first. You're the one who's so adamant we leave. What would you do with them?" He jabbed a rigid finger at me.

"And what would you do if we stayed, Ken? You'd kill them, wouldn't you?" I said.

"I never said that."

"You don't have to. Wouldn't be the first time you've talked about killing someone, would it?" I cast a quick glance toward Gina to let her know I was talking about her.

"You what?" Gina said.

"Well what would you do?" Ken raised his voice. He pushed my shoulder. "Come on. This was all your doing. You've been harping on all about how this is your escape and your idea. Your decision to take this house. Come on, make a tough decision for once. If it's like you say, then the road to Scotland's just as good as anywhere else. It's all crawling with Greens and Hunters and every other sod who'd rather see us swinging from a lamppost than go back to the Workfarms. The whole country is. So come on then, answer me. You can't do it, can you? This is a joke this is. You can't make a real decision."

"Don't you dare give me that shit, Ken. I've been making your decisions for you since the beginning. You wouldn't even be here if it wasn't for me. Look what I've done for you." I held up my bandaged hand.

"Oh really? I don't recall asking you to."

"I should have just given you your five."

"Yes, you should have. Well now's your chance, boyo." Ken said. He stuck his chin out and pointed to the target. "Just imagine McCarthy's standing behind you with his secateurs ready."

The urge to deck him was coursing through my arms, turning my hands into fists. His face was right there in front of me. A nice, big, smug, deserving target. My fists were clenched so tight it hurt. This was my chance. Right here and now, and I was letting it go by doing absolutely nothing. He deserves it. He's been goading me ever since the breakout. Belittling me. I lost a finger thanks to this bastard. Do it.

I moved in front of him. He stuck his chin out further.

Do it.

I wanted to pull my fist back.

Do it, for god sake.

I didn't do it. I couldn't do it. Christ, what the hell was I?

Ken shook his head and tutted. He gave me a big smirk just like McCarthy did that day. "That's what I thought. Just like in Nelson. No bottle. You won't act."

"Yeah? Neither of you two thought of breaking free. You'd all still be at the farm, getting your heads kicked in just for looking at them funny. I saved us from them. At least I tried." I said, shaking from the anger pent up inside me.

"Break free?" Ken laughed the way a teacher would at a kid throwing a strop. "You call this free? I don't feel very free, do you Gina?"

She didn't say anything. She was still stewing over the murder plot.

"What, you thought killing a few dogs and hopping over a wire fence would make you a free man? Wake up, boy. You'll be on the run for the rest of your life at this rate. This 'safe place' idea of yours is a fantasy. Always has been."

"Then why have you been following me?" I said.

"Convenience."

"Oh fuck off." I wanted to hit him again, but the truth was, he was right. He'd said out loud what had been in the back of my mind the whole time, from the school to the protest to now. That voice of doubt, whispering the real reason I hadn't gone off on my own. This entire journey had been pointless.

"All that talk with that woman about your life being borrowed. Well guess what, mate? If you think like that, then your entire freedom was borrowed. If they can come and take it off you, you never had it in the first place. Nobody's free." Ken said.

"Fine. Whatever. I don't care." I said absently. Ken's words had ripped right through me. I felt empty. All the anger gone. I relaxed my fists and I sighed, looking out the window at the driveway and the posh houses beyond it. It was raining. The snow was melting into grey sludge. I sighed again as I realised the futility of everything I'd done. Ken and Gina could do what they liked. We weren't a group any more. I had no reason to pretend to care about them. They were just as ungrateful as each other.

Gina waited until me and Ken had finished arguing. "Right, me and Jimmy are off." She headed for the hallway, but Ken got in her way.

"You're not taking the boy." He said.

"I beg your pardon?" She said.

"I won't repeat myself."

"And since when did you two give a shit about either or us?" Gina said, pointing between me and Ken.

"Since Jimmy became leverage over you. We're keeping him here, because if you take him, there's nothing to stop you letting slip to the Greens that we're here."

Gina laughed. "Oh come off it. You really think I'd do that? I only escaped with you two, for god sake. Jimmy's mine to look after. You two won't do it."

"I don't care. You're not taking him."

Gina turned away and muttered to herself, then turned back. "Well he's going to need some more medicine." She said.

"I'm sure there'll be some in this house somewhere. They've got everything else."

I hated Ken for acting like this house was some sort of treasure trove he'd just dug up out of the blue. If there was medicine here it was because that family tied up in the next room needed it.

"I've already looked and there isn't. He needs antibiotics." Gina said.

"Well you won't be able to get that without knocking off a chemist. And don't expect us to help." Ken pointed at me and him like we were still on the same side.

"Get out of my way then. I'll go get some." Gina tried to shove her way past, but at more than a foot shorter than him and a few stone lighter, she didn't have the leverage to move him.

"Hang on. Why are you in such a rush to leave all of a sudden? The boy's asleep upstairs isn't he?"

"To. Get. Him. Some. Medicine."

"Or maybe you and him have got plans elsewhere, eh?" Ken folded his arms and looked down at Gina the same way he'd look at me when he suggested we murder her.

"I'm not standing for this again. You two are just as bad as each other. I'm going. So is Jimmy. And we're not coming back."

"None of you are going anywhere." Ken said to the pair of us.

"You what?" I said.

"And what are you going to do to stop me?" Gina said.

"Oh I can stop you." Ken unfolded his arms and raised his fists.

She shoved and tried to get past him, but again she barely moved him. Ken grabbed her shoulders and pinned her against the wall. I tried to get him off her, but I wasn't strong enough either. Gina scratched his arms and dug her nails into him.

As Ken raised his fist, Gina shoved her knee up into his groin. His grip released in the moment of agony as he staggered back, nursing his groin and wincing at the pain. Gina took the opportunity and ran. I tried to follow and called out for her to stop, but by the time I was in the hallway, she was already out the front door. The door was swinging open in the wind. Gina looked back at me from the driveway. She had no coat on and already the rain was soaking her clothes, then she ran. I didn't go after her. I didn't help Ken neither. Natalie and Jonathan were making a racket in the other room, but they stopped when I walked in. The way Natalie looked at me told me she'd heard the entire conversation. She must have known my plan to leave wasn't going to happen now. I could hear Ken in the other room, still huffing and cursing to himself. I wanted to tell her something good, but all I could think of was how naïve I'd been for thinking I could be free somewhere. I hated myself for believing it even existed in the first place.

Now that the belief was gone though, I dreaded what was to come.

7

Gina never came back. I waited by the window in the empty living room all day until it got dark, all the while asking myself what I was still doing here? In that time, a couple of Green vans drove past the house. They didn't stop though. They wouldn't around here.

I made a sandwich and sat down on the couch near Natalie and Jonathan. Ken hadn't moved from the chair near the telly since this morning. He hadn't said anything either. His fists sat clenched on the leather arms. A permanent scowl on his face. He kept flicking through the news channels. Natalie and Jonathan looked at me. They were deathly quiet. Terrified to even breathe too loud. There was far too much tension in the room, and it was all coming from Ken. One thing we hadn't considered was Natalie and Jonathan using the bathroom. Natalie had already urinated and soaked her pyjamas and the carpet, and because the heating was on full-whack, the smell of it was in the stuffy air. When I noticed, I mentioned it to Ken. He made a slight noise to show he'd heard me, but he didn't even take his eyes off the news.

I knew that if I left now, I'd be condemning Natalie and Jonathan to death. And I'd picked this house...

"Look at this." Ken pointed to the telly. The news was saying they'd caught one of the Smithybridge Four. He was apprehended stealing medicine from the paediatric ward in Pendle Community Hospital in Nelson, apparently. Shaky footage showed the protester, Marc being carted through a crowd of screaming people by two Hunters. The uniformed Greens were struggling to keep the crowds off him.

"I warned him, the bloody idiot." Ken said.

I didn't say anything. Natalie and Jonathan looked at me again. Now that she'd seen the lies on the news for herself, maybe she'd believe me.

"If she tries to come back, she's not joining us again." Ken said.

"You gonna kill her if she tries?" I said.

"I'll do what's necessary."

I sighed.

"I think Gina had somewhere to be, don't you?" He said.

"What?"

"Yesterday night. She wouldn't tell us how she made it through Nelson. She was awfully cagey about it all. I think the boy and her have been speaking to the Greens."

"Because the Greens are known to be a compromising bunch? Never saw them as the negotiating type."

"She's up to something and that boy will know what it is."

"I don't doubt she's hiding something, but-"

"So let's go find out what it is."

Ken got up and marched up the stairs. I followed him up to Jonathan's bedroom where Ken shoved the door open and flicked the light on. Jimmy was asleep. His dirty, smelly clothes piled on the floor next to the bed.

Ken pulled the duvet off him and Jimmy woke up. He was sleeping naked. He'd had a shower and washed the grime off himself, but he still smelled sickly. He was almost as pale as the bedding.

"Right, boy, it's time for you to talk." Ken said as he grabbed Jimmy's ankle and dragged down the bed towards him. Jimmy was delirious and still half asleep. He feebly tried to shake his foot loose.

"Tell you what, Ken, I'll take this." I said.

"Oh really?" He raised an eyebrow at me. "Willing to get your hands dirty all of a sudden?"

"We shouldn't leave Natalie and Jonathan alone."

"Suit yourself." He said. He let go of Jimmy and went back downstairs. "Have fun."

"Prick." I said to myself once the bedroom door was shut.

Jimmy stared at me, wide eyed like a fish on a hook, not realising I may have just saved his life.

I gave him the duvet back and sat down on the side of the bed. The closer I got to him, the more I could smell the sickness. It was on his breath and in his skin and in his hair. It was even on the sheets.

"Gina's gone, Jimmy. She ran off. The group's broken. Ken's in charge now. I don't know what's going to happen to you, me, that family downstairs. Ken came in here to interrogate you and find out what you were up to yesterday. He seems to think you and Gina have been speaking to the Greens. Truth be told, I'm a little curious as well, because Gina's been so cagey about it." I let out a long and weary sigh. "You're best off telling me what happened now, or Ken will come back and I won't be able to stop him."

He started crying. He coughed again. More blood on his hands. I got him a tissue.

"Jimmy, where were you and Gina planning to go, and how did you get through Nelson yesterday?"

He went to say something, but stopped.

"Please. I'm doing this for you."

"I can't tell you." He croaked.

"Did she speak to any Greens? Make any phone calls?"

"No."

"So it can't be that important then. Why can't you tell me?"

He rolled over and turned his back to me. "Because of what you'll do if you find out."

"What do you mean?"

He refused to talk. I turned him around and asked again, but he still wouldn't say.

"Jimmy, I don't know what Ken will do to you if you don't tell me, so consider this your last chance."

He tried to turn away again, but I wouldn't let him. As I went to Jonathan's wardrobe, I told myself he'd rather it be me doing this than Ken. I repeated it again as I took out a wire coat-hanger and straightened it out. What I did with it, I did for Jimmy's own protection.

Rather me than Ken.
Rather me than Ken.

The blood washed off easy. The soap lathered into a pinkish foam that rinsed off straight away under the hot tap. Even the bits under my nails didn't take too much scrubbing. His screams though... I'd never forget those.

"Rather me than Ken." I'd said it so many times in the last half hour the words had lost all meaning. I was in Natalie's en suite bathroom. The bathroom and both bedroom doors were shut and I could still hear Jimmy crying through them. I didn't deserve to forget the sound.

"Nobody is coming to help you, Jimmy, so tell me now."

My hands were clean, but I picked up the bar of soap again for the fourth, maybe fifth time. The water was scolding hot.

"She's abandoned you, Jimmy. Tell me what you know now, or I'll do it again."

"Why?"

"Because it'll save your life."

"What, so you and Ken can kill me later on?"

A glob of Jimmy's blood was on the sleeve of Jonathan's hoody. I took it off and dumped it in the wash basket, then, resting on the sink, I stared into the mirror and was disgusted at what I saw looking back.

"Tell me what you were doing in Nelson yesterday, Jimmy, or I'll keep going 'til you run out of fingernails."

"Stop acting like you care about me. Gina's the only person who does. She, she looks after me. Keeps you two from leaving me as bait to keep the Greens off your back. We're going up to Scotland to live with her auntie."

I went through to the hallway and put my ear against Jonathan's bedroom door. Jimmy was still sobbing and mewling Gina's name. I'd given him some tissues to wrap up his fingers and stop the bleeding, but there wasn't anything I could give him for the pain.

"Talk now."

"Gina said I shouldn't tell you."

"Why, what's she planning to do to us?"

"Nothing."

"Then tell me."

"I had a seizure."

"What?"

I ran back to the en suite and threw up in the toilet, then slid down the wall and sat on the linoleum floor. I covered my ears, but I could still hear the scream he made as his fingernail cracked.

"She told me I collapsed and had a fit. She looked after me. She was so scared I was going to die. And now she's gone, I will. She said not to tell you, because you and Ken would abandon us... I don't want to die. Please god."

Rather me than Ken.

Well done, Ken. You'd made me into your weapon, just like McCarthy did.

I put a clean t-shirt on and went back to the bedroom door and whispered that I was sorry through the wood. I daren't open it. I couldn't bring myself to see him, to look at what I'd done. He was still sobbing, still nursing his fingers. I said it again, but he didn't reply.

I deserved his silence.

Going back downstairs to the living room, Natalie and Jonathan looked at me, eyes wide in terror. They'd heard it all, and they both stared at the bloody coat-hanger in my hand as I took it into the kitchen and binned it. Natalie sobbed. Jonathan was trying not to.

Ken was in the chair again, flicking through the news channels. Probably been there the whole time. He turned around. "So, what were they planning?"

8

The creaking of hinges in the hallway woke me up. It paused after the first creak, then continued. A gust of wind and a cold draught followed it. It creaked again as the front door closed. Lying still, I listened to footsteps move along the hall and go up the stairs. They went straight to Jonathan's bedroom, which told me all I needed to know. Before she came back down I got up off the couch and waited in the hallway.

"What are you doing here, Gina?" I said as I flicked the lights on.

She startled and shielded her eyes from the light.

"Where is he?" She said. She gripped a kitchen knife in her hand. She must have got it from somewhere while she was gone. Her hair, face, and clothes were soaking wet.

"He isn't upstairs." I said.

"Where is he then?" She whispered.

I took a step towards her, hands up as a gesture of peace and she stuck the knife out at me. I stopped. The point was only a few inches away.

"I'm just going to show you." I said.

"Do it then."

I showed her to the main living room where Jimmy was laid on the carpet beside to the Monroes. Ken had refused to untie them and still refused to let them use the bathroom. The room stank now. Ken was still in the chair. They were all awake now that the light was on.

"I'm taking him." Gina said. I moved out of her way as she entered the living room.

"Well aren't you going to stop her?" Ken said to me.

"Shut it, old man." Gina pointed her knife at him. No, I wasn't.

"Is this part of your deal with them?" Ken said as he got up off the chair. "You get to keep the boy if you lead them to us?"

113

"What are you on about? What deal?"

"Oh come off it, Gina. You've been running us around since the start. I wouldn't be surprised if they let us escape just so you could be their plant." Ken said. I'd told him what Jimmy said about him collapsing, but he didn't believe it. He said he would have a go at Jimmy himself first thing in the morning and get the real truth out of him.

"Say what you like. I don't care." Gina said. I was surprised. Earlier today a comment like that from Ken would have started a tirade of jibes and arguments between them. She spoke now like she'd had enough of all that. She wasn't playing games and she wasn't interested in what we thought. She was here for Jimmy. She'd come to rescue him from us. Too late for that. Jimmy stood up and as he approached her, she saw his hands. "What the hell have you done to him?" She unwrapped the bloody tissues off his fingers. The bottom layer had clotted and stuck in between the cracks in his nails as the blood had dried. He winced as she ran her finger over them. "You bastard." She glared at Ken.

Jimmy wrapped his arms around her and put his head against her shoulder. He sobbed and thanked her for coming for him.

"We're leaving. You two can do whatever the hell you like." Gina said.

"I've already told you what's what." Ken said. "I'm staying here. The boy's staying here. We're all staying here, except you."

"Wrong." I said. I walked over to Natalie and Jonathan, avoiding Gina and her big knife.

"Oh you can't be serious." Ken said, giving me that condescending amusement look again.

"We're all leaving right now. You included, Ken. This is their house. We were looking for an empty one, remember?"

"Not this again. Still believing in fairy tales are we?" He said.

Jonathan looked at me with such hatred that I was afraid to untie him. Natalie first. Get her on my side, then she can talk her son down.

"We're not monsters, Ken." I said.

"But we are criminals. We may as well act like it."

"I'm not a criminal." I said.

"Explain that to Jimbo then, or them two. What have we been running for then? They say we are on the telly, they say we are in parliament. It's time you drop the frothy idealism and realise. They say we're criminals, and they make the rules, so like it or not, we're criminals." Ken said. He grabbed hold of Jimmy's arm.

Right then, all of us turned round as a window smashed in the kitchen. A second later another smashed in the front door.

"Oh my god, they've-" Whatever she was about to say, I'd never know. Gina's words were cut off by a high pitched shriek and two searing white lights erupting from the hallway and the kitchen. I tried to cover my eyes, but I was too slow. I fell to my knees with my eyes burning and my hands clasped over my ears. It was over in seconds and when the sound shrank back I could hear commotion all around me. I felt around, seeing nothing but blazing white as I tried desperately to make it to the door. As my eyesight returned, shapes gradually took form in the light, and I made out the blurry image of Ken fleeing upstairs, a Hunter right behind him.

Gina. So she did screw us. She must have. Ken was right. I looked for her through the blur and saw her holding on to Jimmy as two Hunters dragged her away from him. The boy stumbled forward as their fingers pulled apart.

One of the Hunters shoved Gina against the fireplace and choked her. As she grasped at the gloved hand around her throat, the other Hunter pulled out a taser and shot her point-blank in the chest with it. They let her go and she collapsed to the floor, where they continued to shock her until foam was pooling out of her mouth.

A window smashed upstairs.

The shank must have fallen out my pocket in the commotion, because Jimmy picked it up off the carpet and ran at the two Hunters on Gina. He barely made it two steps before two more Hunters intercepted him from the hallway. They charged at him, their armoured shoulders knocking him off his feet, sending him sprawling to the floor. They stood on his arms to keep him down as they each took out a crowbar and took turns on him. He cried out once, then went quiet. The Hunters carried on, not a word from either of them.

"I surrender, I surrender." I shouted. I got on my knees and put my hands behind my head. A Hunter that was untying Natalie came over and stood me up. Enormous in all that black and green armour and not a single piece of flesh showing. All I could see in that black mask was my own reflection, but I could hear his heavy breathing through the small vent holes in either cheek. He tied my hands behind my back with a cable tie, then he pulled his gloved fist back and hooked me across the chin. Before I could recover, he'd swung a crowbar into my ribs. My legs gave out and I spat blood on the floor, but he wouldn't let me drop. He had hold of my shoulder and made sure I stayed standing as he carried on. We'd killed one of them. Broken their image and proved it could be done. He owed it to his fallen comrade, and they all owed it to their reputation. They were supposed to be feared, and now thanks to us that might not happen, so an example had to be set. We had to become a cautionary tale. No one else must get the brilliant idea of following us. They wanted people to remember what happened to the Smithybridge Four any time someone thought of fighting back. They'd think again, then fall back in line. Do as they were told. With each swing of the crowbar and every bone that broke, that message became more acute. Even though I couldn't see any of him, I could tell he was enjoying it.

When he finally did let me fall he kicked me in the stomach until I coughed up more blood.

The Hunter dragged me out into the hallway by my ankle and forced me to stand up against the wall. They were already bagging Jimmy's body up and Gina had been taken away. A Hunter came trudging down the stairs alone. No Ken. Either he was dead too, or he'd gotten away. The way the Green slouched and plodded down the stairs suggested the latter.

Back in the living room, Natalie threw her arms around the Hunter that untied her and Jonathan, sobbing and thanking him for saving her life. I called to her and tried to tell her I was sorry, but it came out as a garbled slur thanks to the dislocated jaw and swollen face. She saw me though, and she went for me. It took three Hunters to hold her back.

Nobody was watching Jonathan as he picked the shank up off the floor near the black bag with Jimmy inside and hid it against his arm. There were eleven people all moving about the living room. So much bustle that he strafed past them and not one of them saw it. They only noticed when he was standing in front of me with the shank held out. One of the Hunters sprang for him. Jonathan swore at me as the Hunter pinned him to the floor. Too late. I looked down at the rake tooth taped to a toothbrush handle that was sticking out of me just to the right of my belly button.

With the realisation came the pain. Hot, then cold as blood trickled out. I could feel the rusted metal scraping against something soft inside. All around the stab wound was on fire. Every wince and movement brought more pain. One of the Hunters grabbed the toothbrush. He twisted it and churned it around inside, grating it against bone. Then he ripped the shank out. I fell down, bleeding on the hardwood floor. Everything blurred.

Before it all went dark I heard Natalie fighting to get the Greens off her son.

9

"It's supposed to be getting lighter in the evenings now." Tom said, leaning over. Martin looked up at the darkening sky and his face wrinkled up.

"Really?"

"I know it hasn't yet, but it will be soon." Tom wrestled a bunch of onions out of the icy soil. They were stuck in tight. The whole field was covered in a layer of frost and the mud had frozen into solid clumps. After a lot of heaving he got them out, then shook the loose clumps of dirt off them and dumped them with the rest in the wheelbarrow Martin was holding. One pulled the crops, the other worked the barrow. That was the way it worked. Every row had a two-man team. Except mine. I was on my own.

"Still frost on the ground. Wind hasn't let up yet. It's going to be cold for another month or so, I reckon, so not sure what good a bit more daylight's going to do." I said to them. They were on the row next to mine, a few feet further ahead. They looked at me, both waiting for the other to speak first. When neither of them did, Tom stepped over to the next bunch of onions and Martin moved his wheelbarrow further up past him. I sighed. I couldn't blame them.

Half an hour later when the fields were lit by floodlights, the klaxons went off back at the compound, signalling the end of the shift. Everyone in the fields turned and looked up the rows at the grey concrete buildings in the centre.

"Christ, thank god for that." Tom said, stretching his lower back out.

"Aye. Come on, let's get inside." Martin said as he steered his wheelbarrow around, leaning into it to get the wheel over a clod of frozen dirt. He looked back at me and saw me standing still, staring at the building. The worry was written on my face. I looked back at him and I could tell he wanted to say something

121

comforting, but for his own reasons he just nodded and carried on. The dread in the pit of my stomach writhed, urging me to not go back. Martin knew what went on. They all knew about it.

The compound was a good three hundred metres away. The ten foot high, barbed wire fence that marked the edge of the farm was closer. I was equal distance between two tower posts. Through the layer of trees planted on the outside of the fence to hide the barbed wire from the public, I could see Smithybridge a few miles away. I looked at the compound, then back at the fence, and escape crossed my mind again. This time it'll be different, I thought, better, just me. My hands tightened on the ice-cold wheelbarrow handles. Out there was something different. A relief.

Freedom.

I sighed. There it was again. That old lie. The one they fed to everyone out there and everyone just swallowed down without question. I'd believed it too until I saw first-hand what freedom really looked like. Ideas only exist at someone else's exception. Why did I keep torturing myself thinking about it? It wouldn't be any different than last time.

The stab wound in my stomach and my hand were hurting. The cold had got to them again and the bandages needed changing. Neither one of them were healing right. They hadn't had the chance to. With a heavy sigh, I grabbed the wheelbarrow handles and started pushing back toward the compound.

McCarthy was waiting by the barn door, shining his torch down on his watch, shaking his head, tutting. He stopped me.

"Hey look here, it's the dead man. Last one back again." He said. He made me wait while the rest of the farmers dumped their harvest, ensuring I was the last one back. As they passed me, each of them he gave me the same look Martin had.

McCarthy looked down at my wheelbarrow. "Not much there, is there, Spartacus?" He said. There was no point in explaining that I was doing a two-man job on my own. As Farm Overseer, it was his idea.

As I was dumping the onions onto the barn floor, the metal doors slid shut and the lights came on. There were more people in the barn now.

"Last one back again. That's what, twelve days in a row now?" Officer Johns said. He wrote it up on his clipboard. "Right then. Against the wall. Hands up. Come on, you know the game by now."

I did as I was told. I knew the game by now. And I knew what happened if I didn't play too.

"Alright lads." McCarthy said. "Ready?" I closed my eyes and tensed my back. "Go."

McCarthy, Johns, Barker and Payne pelted me with the onions that I and the other farmers had spent all day picking. One of them hit the back of my knee and I dropped. Johns cheered. He'd just won himself a free drink.

Barker tutted. "You know the rules, Spartacus." I hated his scouse accent. It made everything sound sarcastic. "You went down again, so..."

So they carried on with truncheons. I didn't crawl away. I didn't fight back. It was easier to let them get it over with. My bowels still hurt from the last time I'd tried to stop them.

When they were done, Barker and Payne, dragged me back to the billet. Johns walked behind us, marking it up on his clipboard. "You made us look bad when you broke out, Spartacus. There were enquiries. Investigations. Some good people lost their jobs on account of you. You won't be doing it again. We'll make sure of it. You ain't going anywhere, buddy." He said, the same as he'd said yesterday and the day before that, and the same as he'd say tomorrow too.

They opened the door and dropped me on the billet doorstep. The farmers stopped playing cards, talking to each other, whatever they were doing, and watched. Some of them shook their heads, some sighed, some glared at the Greens in a quiet rage. All of them doing the exact same thing when McCarthy cut my finger off and they did nothing then either. They all made a point to look elsewhere when Barker and Payne looked back at them. Useless. Absolutely useless.

"See you tomorrow, Spartacus." Barker said as he shut the door on his way out.

I rolled over onto my back and lie there while the pain subsided as much as it ever would subside. The farmers were still watching me. The silence in the room was heavy. Someone at the back coughed and it felt like an interruption.

I crawled on my hands and knees over to my cot in the corner. Ben Owens moved a table out of my way, but other than that, nobody had any intention of helping. They may have wanted to, but for their own self-preservation, they didn't.

Living under the Greens and the conditions on the Workfarm, the farmers had become a tight-knit community. They shared food to make sure everyone got an equal measure, if someone was under the day's quota, those who were over would give some of theirs, they carried each other to their beds after recalibrations, washed and dressed wounds, changed bandages, shared the right answers for the nightly Q&A. They did what they could for each other to make it through. New farmers adapted quickly to this system, and even the most stubborn person learned that being out for themselves wasn't going to get them far.

When Payne and McCarthy dumped me on the billet floor on my first day back, one guy, Adam his name was, tried to help me up. McCarthy stood watching while Payne beat Adam to the floor. He made sure everybody saw it, everybody heard it, and more importantly, everybody understood. The message was clear: I was on my own. Excluded from the community. I did not exist.

As I got nearer my bunk, the farmers went back to their own thing. Show was over. Next showing at the same time tomorrow. The bunk itself was three planks of wood that were only a bit wider than my shoulders. The mattress was so thin I could feel them underneath it. It smelled of other people's sweat and was covered in stains.

I took off my shirt and untied the bandages around my waist and hand, then laid flat on my back and let the air get to them. The stab wound was purple and pink and smelled like off cheese. It would weep clear liquid sometimes. I'd been draining it into the sink in the mornings, but it was growing. The hand was no better. It'd gotten no worse either, antibiotics saw to that, but I didn't see that as a plus. It wasn't like the finger would grow back and the black parts of the stump were still soft and flaking off. It hadn't taken the Green doctor long to declare me good for work. A week spent in a hospital tent erected on the farm grounds, then a quick once over. Here're some bandages, here're some antibiotics, off you pop.

I closed my eyes and listened to the radio in the far corner. Clive Montgomery was being interviewed live.

"It was a terrible thing what happened and uh, I'm glad I could be a part of uh, helping to stop their crime wave."

"And were you scared at all? I mean, what these people did to Adam Braithwaite was so horrendous that there must have been a point in the back of your mind that thought 'OK, I could get seriously hurt here'."

"Well yeah, I mean, danger's an occupational hazard, so you mentally prepare for it. I mean, I've had lots of combat training, martial arts, strength training, and uh, mental training, that teaches you to forget about the fear. It just kicks in and takes over. It becomes second nature really."

"That's amazing, Mr Montgomery. Absolutely amazing. Now, may I ask, have you seen the headlines today?"

"No."

"Well this one here is a quote from Mrs Braithwaite, the widow of Adam Braithwaite. It just says 'I'm glad they're dead' in rather large lettering. What do you think of that?"

"I think that all life is precious, but after what they did to her husband, she deserves some justice. I can see her point of view. I mean, they killed her husband, you know?"

"I suppose you're front page now as well aren't you? What do your kids think about you being all over the tabloids, 'cause I understand you're a father as well?"

"Ha ha well, they just can't believe it. They ran off to school that morning shouting 'Daddy's a hero, daddy's a hero'. They've gotten a real kick out of it."

"And what do you think? Come on, don't tell me you're not the least bit chuffed about it as well."

"Well, it's all still a bit new at the minute. Couple of weeks ago I was just a family man living on a street. Today I still feel like a family man, but now people come up to me in the street and ask to shake my hand."

"And do you feel like a hero?"

"Not really. I just do my job like everybody else. Heroes are out in the Middle-East and uh, out every day, rain or shine, collecting money for cancer research and stuff."

"You're so modest. Isn't he so modest, listeners? I can't believe how modest you are. I think you're a hero. You're my hero, and I'm sure many of those listening will agree."

"Oh, well thank you very much."

"In case you've just tuned in, I'm Matt Willis and I'm here with Clive Montgomery who, as you may already know by now, single-handedly apprehended the remaining three of the Smithybridge Four five weeks ago. All of which were killed in the confrontation-"

"-Uh, I tried to save them."

"Sorry?"

"I said I tried to save them."

"How do you mean?"

"Well, after we'd rescued the Monroe family, we'd picked up their trail on a bridge and we had them cornered. They tried to fight us off and when they realised they couldn't, they all jumped off the bridge and committed suicide."

"They took the coward's way out?"

"Yeah. Coward's way out. I'd have liked them to go through the court system. That's what it's there for, but you know, these people. Like you said. Cowards."

"Blimey. Terrible... So, Clive, what's this I saw on the Twitter grapevine about you having an autobiography currently being fast-tracked for an Easter release?"

"Oh yes, well, I got a call from this fella at a publishing house-I can't say which one at the moment I'm afraid, who said they're interested in publishing a book of my life story. I was a bit funny about it at first, because I think I'm quite ordinary. A bit tea and biscuits, you know, but they assured me that these days people want to know their heroes personally, so it'd be good to have an autobiography about the average man."

"And I bet they offered you a fat stack of money too, am I right? We all know you authors make tons."

"Well, they offered me an advance, quite a hearty one, but you know, the money's not important. I've got my family, my house, a decent job. Money won't change all that. Well, it might go towards the mortgage. I'm going to keep on working though. Keep paying tax, supporting the nation. That's important."

"Modest to a tee. How great is Clive, eh listeners? So, can I ask, what are your thoughts on the Smithybridge Four, now that you've seen them face to face?"

"I think they're cowards."

"Yeah?"

"Yeah. They beat an innocent man to death for what, doing his job, then they go and take a poor family hostage. All Adam was trying to do was keep them safe, you know? Safety Officer at the farm. It's like, they're ungrateful for the opportunity. They knew about the shortages, about their responsibilities to the country. They're still going now. Shops are emptying out. I read yesterday that Filey's become a ghost town, because there's not enough food to go around and so has Driffield. They're the worst kind of scum for doing what they've done, especially at this time. Opportunity was handed to them on a plate and they chucked it all away. And what they did to that poor Monroe family..."

"Strong words there from the man of the hour. Anyway we're gonna take a break for a few minutes. You're listening to Matt Willis and Clive Montgomery. Here's some music for you all."

Some of the guys were looking at me, waiting for me to chip in. I rolled onto my side and faced the wall as I massaged the bruises on my legs.

Christ, they really knew how to lay it on thick. Gushing with all that 'saintly grafter' modesty. Squeeze that last bit of hate out of people so they can tell Tony Bennett he was right and nod along with whatever he has planned next. The embargoes were still going. I'd heard on the radio the other day that even some parts of Greater Manchester were emptying out. Food rationing was being considered, because the Workfarms' output wasn't up to scratch. I'd seen this Clive Montgomery in the papers too and he was no Hunter. Too fat to fit in the uniform for a start. He looked like Fred Flintstone. Another stooge to feed people a story just like on the news. His autobiography would be some ghost-written, working-class hero anecdote about how he'd worked all his life and paid his dues and how much people like us offended him. He'd end up on Celebrity Big Brother eventually, living large on a lie.

We were all dead now, the four of us. They said we were, and they made the rules, so like it or not, we were. Being legally dead meant they couldn't afford to let me go. I was too much of a liability. I'd talk. People would notice I existed. The others were dead for real for all I knew. Jimmy was. Christ, out of all of us, he didn't deserve it. Ken... I couldn't believe he might have gotten away. And Gina, well, she had it coming. Did she make a deal with the Hunters, or did they just follow her hoping she'd lead them to us? It didn't matter. I should have got out on my own. I shouldn't have picked that house. I should have stood up to Ken sooner. Hell, I shouldn't have even left in the first place. At least that way the Monroe's lives wouldn't have been ruined and Jimmy might not have died.

I could still hear his screams. They kept me awake most nights. I closed my eyes and put my hands over my ears, but Jimmy kept sobbing until I did too.

It was minus three at morning roll call. Six am, standing in a line outside the billet, and still dark. The flood lights were on, but so much snow was blowing in, you couldn't even see the fences.

Everyone but me was given a coat. Then Payne went down the line and gave everyone a woolly hat. My fingernails were already blue and I was shivering when he got to me. He dropped the hat on the frozen mud and told me I'd better pick it up.

When roll call was done, the gates were opened and a line of fresh faces walked in. You could tell they were newly caught. They all look sullen and sheepish. Their clothes were clean and their faces were washed. As they lined up in front of us, they stared at us, shocked at what they saw. We were thin, gaunt, weather worn and bruised. Some of them understood straight away and they were terrified. We were what they were going to become, everything they'd heard about this place was false, this wasn't some plucky opportunity to feed the nation and save kiddies lives, we weren't grateful for the chance to pay back our debt to the society, everything they'd seen on telly was a lie. One of them, a young lad with curly hair, tried to run. He got as far as the Hunter's van that had brought them here when he was tackled by Barker. He and McCarthy picked him up and shoved him into the barn. His first recalibration. Better to get it over with early. Saves him being afraid of the next one.

I faced forward. The wind was loud enough to mask the sounds coming from the barn. With any luck he'd learn the first time round. Not likely, but I suppose I couldn't talk. It cost me a hell of a lot more before I'd understood. I got the message now though. I'd paid for it with Jimmy's life.

The newbies were ordered to face the fields. Poor bastards. They all had colour in their cheeks and meat on their bones. All except for one of them.

One at the very far end was hard-faced and thin. Already worn down to nothing. Stood straight, face forward, shivering, hair shaved right down to the scalp, black eyes and a bust lip. I tried to get a good look at the face, but the others kept getting in the way. I coughed a few times to get people to turn around, but that one never did. They didn't look anywhere but straight ahead. Soon everybody was split into pairs, one given a fork and the other a wheelbarrow and assigned a row. I was given both duties again, and so was the person at the end of the newbie row.

Just who the hell was it?

I had to know. I kept looking over whilst I was pulling onions, but I was too far away to make out the face. They looked nervous though, always looking around when nobody else was watching. Maybe they knew I was making an effort to look? Maybe it was just me staring at them that made them nervous? I didn't care. I had to know who it was. An hour or so into the work I stuck my fork in the ground and limped over. I could feel everyone watching me, Greens included, as I cut straight across the rows.

134

This would mean a recalibration for definite, but what was new? I had to know. The newbie wasn't looking. Too busy struggling with the wheelbarrow. I grabbed them by their bony shoulder. She startled and spun around. She recognised me in an instant and was terrified. I clenched my fist.

"Told you we'd never make it up to Scotland." I said.